D0409086

083858

x    Maggio, Rosalie

        box Christmas.

083858

x Christmas.

**Colusa County Free Library**

738 Market Street
Colusa, CA   95932
Phone : 458-7671

# The Music Box Christmas

# The Music Box Christmas

## ROSALIE MAGGIO

MORROW JUNIOR BOOKS / NEW YORK

12.95

Printed in the United States of America.

1  2  3  4  5  6  7  8  9  10

Library of Congress Cataloging-in-Publication Data
Maggio, Rosalie.
The music box Christmas / Rosalie Maggio.
p.  cm.  90B10122
Summary: Despite his grandmother's recent death and the return of
his troublesome father, Nick determines to find a way for the family
to have a real Christmas celebration.
ISBN 0-688-08851-1 (trade)
[1. Christmas—Fiction.  2. Family problems—Fiction.]  I. Title.
PZ7.M2726Mu  1990
[Fic]—dc20      90-38529      CIP      AC

*To DAVID*
*Liz, Katie, Matt*

# CHAPTER ONE

# ✳ *December 20*

"Christmas is coming, the goose is getting fat. Please put a penny in the old man's—"

I turned off the radio so hard that the little button flipped up in the air and bounced across the kitchen shelf. Through the window, I could see snow piled nearly to the top of the fence, and more of it frosting all the roofs and trees. On my way home from school, I noticed that everybody but the grouchy Bensons had Christmas trees up. Stores were full of Christmas decorations, there were Christmas specials on TV, and at school today we'd spent our whole art class working on Christmas presents. So I knew Christmas was coming . . . for everybody else.

The calendar on the cupboard door said December 20. But you'd never have known it, judging by our house. It looked like one of those cabins up in the mountains where the old prospector has died and the mice and spiders have taken over. Gloom and neglect were everywhere. The gloom was probably due to the fact that somebody had lowered all the window shades the day Gabby died and nobody had bothered to raise them again. The neglect was easy to understand: Gabby had always taken care of everything, but she wasn't here anymore.

Dirty breakfast dishes trailed all over the counter, dust balls skated along the floor every time the front door opened, and the kitchen floor was so sticky we were lucky not to be permanently bonded to it. Worst of all was the silence—we were all tiptoeing around as if we were waiting for something. I knew now we weren't waiting for Christmas.

Yesterday when I hinted to Ma that we really ought to start getting ready for Christmas, she gave me a long, reproachful look. I knew she was grieving for Gabby—we all were—so maybe it was insensitive of me. But later I wondered why I'd backed off. Christmas was going to come no matter what happened. We couldn't just ignore it, could we?

"Nick! Rudy took his clothes off again!" called my little sister, Christa.

I didn't even try to wake Peabody. Peabody was the new baby-sitter, who went to night school, studied late, and then spent the next day at our house catching up on sleep. I stepped over Peabody's outstretched legs and then stopped to wonder for about the fiftieth time whether Peabody was a boy or a girl. Patched jeans, several layers of sweaters, a denim jacket, hair just below the ears: It was anybody's guess. I suppose Peabody was okay. If the house was on fire, Peabody would wake up and get us out of there—I think. But I sure missed Gabby. In a grandma contest, she would have won maybe first or second place.

Wearing nothing but a diaper, my baby brother, Rudy, grinned up at me and blinked his big blue eyes. I had had a lot of practice dressing him since he was born a little over a year ago, so I forked the kid into his clothes in a couple of minutes flat. But as I was snapping the last snap, Rudy was untying his left shoelace.

"Come on, Rudy, gimme a break," I said. "At least wait until I get you dressed before you start undressing again."

Rudy smiled and reached for his right shoe. Apparently he didn't feel the situation called for either of the two words he knew how to say. Gabby had been teaching Rudy to undress and dress himself, but she had gotten only halfway through the job. I wondered who would teach Rudy to put his clothes back on.

I stood up and backed into Christa. "Oh, Christa, I didn't see you."

"Typical," said Christa. "Nobody sees me. Except Primrose." From the safety of Christa's arms, Primrose the rabbit gave me one of her smug looks. I'd never thought rabbits were very smart, but this one can read minds. She knows exactly what I think of her.

"I'll bet I don't even get any Christmas presents," said Christa, looking around the room. I looked, too. We had never lived in one place for as long as two years before, and I loved the feeling of knowing a place by heart. It wasn't the greatest house in the world—the wallpaper was peeling in places, and we didn't have much furniture—but every morning when I got up, everything was the same as when I'd gone to bed. It hadn't always been like that. When I was *really* little, Ma and Dad didn't even wake me up when we moved. They just carried me, still sleeping, from one place to another.

For once, I would have liked a little less of the sameness—some Christmas decorations, for example.

Although I didn't usually like being that close to Primrose, I put my arm around Christa and said gently, "I suppose when you're only eight years old, getting Christmas presents seems pretty important, hmmm?"

Christa threw my arm off and said, "Nick Latimer, you're a fathead, you know that?" She fixed me with screwed-up little eyes and said, "You can keep your smarmy old big brother talk. You want Christmas presents just as much as I do."

Christa reminds me of Big John. According to the song, Big John was quiet and shy, but if you spoke to him at all, you only said hi. I don't argue with shy, quiet Christa when she's mad—and especially not when she's got that sharp-toothed rabbit in her arms. So I said, "Well, maybe I do, but what difference does it make what we want? I don't think we're having Christmas this year."

While Rudy peeled off another layer of clothes and Christa sniffed quietly, I stared at the living room and thought how it ought to look this time of year. The only sign of Christmas was the music box on the mantel. Its dark, polished wood was decorated with gold scrollwork and dim paintings of the first Christmas. When the lid was raised, seven tiny angels slowly stood and began playing "Joy to the World."

We had spent every Christmas for as far back as I could remember with Gabby, and the music box had always played. Gabby had kept it in her secret cave of a room and brought it out only at Christmastime. One of the last things she had done before she died was to set it on the fireplace mantel and say with satisfaction, "There, now. It won't be long until Christmas. Tomorrow we start the baking."

That was right after lunch on December 5. I remember everything about that day. It was a Saturday, which meant that Gabby was getting ready for her afternoon at the grocery store. Ma used to say that you couldn't *pay* most people to go to Dennick's on Saturday because it was so crowded, but that's why Gabby went—it was a big party to her. She and her friends would stand around blocking the aisles, laughing and talking. I know, because I went with her once.

It was torture. We wouldn't see her again until late Saturday afternoon, when she'd come find me and say, "Nick, will you help me get the shopping cart up the back stairs? I'd do it myself, but I bought one can of soup too many today."

But on that Saturday, Gabby put on her long gray-green tweed coat that was about a hundred years old . . . and then took it off again. Laying it with her purse on the bed, she wandered from her room to the living room, from her room to the kitchen. On one of her trips, she brought out the music box. She put her coat back on, then took it off again. Finally, smiling a little shakily, she said she was going to lie down for a bit before going for the groceries.

I heard her, but I didn't hear her, if you know what I mean. Powderhorn Lake had just been declared safe for ice skating, and a bunch of us were meeting there that afternoon. I didn't have ice skates, and ever since lunch I'd been calling around to see if I could borrow a pair. By the time I remembered the Maki family down the street who had about five kids and would lend you anything, Gabby had gone to her room.

We skated and fooled around at Powderhorn until dark, and I remember laughing and racing across the ice like a runaway bowling ball. I say bowling ball because once, when I couldn't stop in time, I ran into a group of kids and I got a strike—all ten of them went down. I'm not usually loud and silly, but there's something about skimming along on skates that makes you feel so free and happy. My finest moment was doing an elaborate fake fall in front of a bunch of girls.

I didn't get home until dark, and I was so wet and cold that I went straight to bed. I wasn't too tired, though, to set one of my shoes outside my bedroom door. I even looked down the hall to be sure Christa had set hers and Rudy's out. She had.

I always looked forward to St. Nicholas Day, partly because it was my name day and partly because it broke up the long wait for Christmas. When I was little, Gabby taught me how *Sinter Claes,* the Dutch words for "St. Nicholas," had become Santa Claus in this country, and how European children put out shoes or hung stockings on the mantel the night before St. Nicholas Day. Later I told the story to Christa, and I suppose she'd told Rudy. It was always Gabby who crept by in the middle of the night or early in the morning (I never caught her at it, although I tried) and filled our shoes with cookies and nuts and maybe a tangerine or a toy whistle or even a yo-yo or a comic book.

When I woke up that December 6, I was in such a hurry to get to my shoe that I dragged half my tangled-up blankets and sheets with me. I whipped open the door and looked down.

The shoe was empty.

I thought at first that it must not be morning yet, but my watch said that not only was it morning, but I'd slept in—

it was nearly nine-thirty. Down the hall, Christa's moccasin and Rudy's sneaker were also still empty.

My next thought was that I had the wrong day. Christa must have gotten the day wrong, too. As it turned out, it was a wrong day, all right, just about the wrongest day you could imagine.

Gabby had died in her sleep of a heart attack sometime during the night. By the time I got up, the ambulance had already taken her away.

I'll never forget Ma's face when we got back from the funeral three days later. My mother is very thin, and with her pale reddish flyaway hair and her freckles, she sometimes looks more like our cousin than our mother. Ma stood just inside the living room door, her long, restless hands smoothing out her gloves, and stared at the music box.

Christa must have noticed Ma's look and, being Christa, she did the wrong thing. She said, "Can we play it now, Ma?"

Ma's voice is usually whispery, but this time it was thin and sharp. "Don't anybody—I mean *anybody*—touch that music box."

It must be terrible when your mother dies. Because it was pretty terrible for me, and Gabby was just my grandmother. I don't really mean "just"—Gabby was a super grandmother. Even my friend Tyrone said so, and he's had five grandmothers to compare her with (it's a long story that has to do with the fact that his parents are really into weddings).

I knew that Ma couldn't think about Christmas because Gabby had just died. But I didn't think Gabby would have wanted it this way. And I was *sure* that she would like us to play her music box.

Christa was waving her hand in front of my face. "Oh, Christa," I said. "Are you still here?"

She looked at me impatiently, but her voice wobbled as she said, "Nick, I don't like it. Everything's awful." Christa isn't a great one for details, but she tunes in the big picture pretty well. It *was* sort of awful around our house, and being Christmastime made it ten times worse.

Ma was either crying or in her room—but since she cried in there, too, it hardly made any difference where she was. Nobody did any housework, so there were clothes and toys all over the furniture and floor, and none of us could find anything. Peabody could have helped out, but if Peabody ever stayed awake long enough to talk, I'm sure the conversation would be something like, "Housework? You expect me to do housework and still get my sleep?"

Worst of all was imagining how things were at other people's houses. I knew they were putting up Christmas trees, baking cookies, getting ready for company, wrapping presents. I wished *we* could have had that. I didn't mind the mess so much. I mostly minded that nobody cared about what was happening to all of us. We were a ship without a captain, a kite without a string, a chicken without a head— well, never mind. You get the idea. And what was happening to us was that Christmas was going to pass us by. So, yes, Christa was right. Things were pretty awful at our house.

But I didn't know just *how* awful until I went to change out of my school clothes. Partly because my room is so small and partly because I'm just a naturally organized person, I keep everything super neat. But today when I opened the closet door, I noticed my shoes weren't lined up the way they usually were. And next to them was a pair of size tens— scuffed old wing tips that I would never forget.

Dad had been drinking the day we went shoe shopping, and when the shoe clerk said those shoes weren't the ones on sale, Dad yelled and blustered and threatened until the clerk gave him the shoes for the sale price. I never could get used to the scenes, which is why I remember the wing tips so well.

Did I mention the worst part about the shoes? There was someone standing in them. My dad was back.

CHAPTER TWO

 *December 20*

(*CONTINUED*)

The best way I can explain my dad is to say he's a lot like
the old nursery rhyme:

> *There was a little girl*
> *Who had a little curl*
> *Right in the middle of her forehead.*
> *When she was good, she was very, very good,*
> *And when she was bad, she was horrid.*

It had been nearly two years since I'd seen my dad, and
I had to study him to see what kind of a mood he was in.
He looked okay, but I remembered that he could change

pretty quickly, so I said, "Hi, Dad," real evenlike, and checked to see how far I was from the door.

"Hey, son!" he said, smiling and untangling himself from my shirts. I relaxed a little. The times to watch out for are when he says, "Listen, kid."

"How've you been? It's good to see you." And he gave me the old bear hug. I'd never liked the old bear hug because I couldn't hug back. And it never really felt like a hug. I just sort of hung there until Dad decided the hug was done.

"So," he said, dropping me, "it's been a while. The thing is, I need a place to stay for a few days. And of course your ma'd never let me stay here if she knew about it. I figure nobody uses the basement much, so I'm going to fix a little hidey hole down there. You can bring me food and let me know when the coast is clear so I can make a few phone calls."

My dad always said I was dumb, and he's probably right. I just stood there staring at him with all the native wit of a coat hanger. I remember one time when I was in the grocery store and I heard two women speaking a foreign language. At first I thought my ears were scrambled or something, and I shook my head to clear them. What they were saying sounded like words, but I couldn't understand them. I felt the same way now while my dad talked.

There I was, thinking about Christmas and Gabby and how sad Ma was, and suddenly my dad—a guy who was in prison, last I heard—was standing in my bedroom talking about hiding out in our basement.

For a minute, I thought about just shutting the closet door and going to the kitchen to get something to eat.

"Uh, gee, Dad," I said, "I don't think that will work, because—"

My dad did one of his quick switches. He lifted me off the ground with a handful of sweatshirt and said, "Listen, kid! It's not your job to think."

He must have read the panic in my eyes because he said, "Yeah, your ma wouldn't like it, would she?"

Wouldn't like it? On top of Gabby's death, that would just about be the last straw for Ma. I remember what it was like before Dad got arrested. It was something we never talked about.

My stomach growled noisily.

"Yeah, me, too, son!" said my dad, smiling again and letting go of my shirt. "Why don't you ride shotgun until I get down in the basement and then bring me something to eat?"

I told Christa and Rudy to go hide and I'd find them. While they were giggling and trying to squeeze under Ma's bed, I checked to see that Peabody was still sleeping. It was easy getting Dad to the basement without anyone seeing him. The hard part was watching him scoop out some dusty old bottles of liquor from the cupboard over the refrigerator on his way down.

"And that's another thing," he said. "I'll need some more booze pretty soon."

I'm thirteen years old, for pete's sake. How does he think

I'm going to get him some booze? But that's my dad. And it's coming back to me pretty quickly that I didn't ever used to ask him questions. About anything.

I watched him as he made a show of tiptoeing down the basement stairs, and I realized this was all sort of a game to him. I don't know if my dad was really grown up or not. Of course, that was the handy thing about him. I remember that when he was in a good mood—and, to be fair, that was about half the time—he was a lot of fun. He used to play board games with me—Chutes and Ladders when I was little, checkers later on. Before he left we were playing a lot of Monopoly, although he wasn't very good at it.

I shut the basement door behind him and went to "find" Rudy and Christa. They were probably hungry, too.

Christa and I poked around in the cupboards, but Gabby hadn't believed in convenience foods and we'd used up just about everything in the refrigerator. Gabby always had scones or granola cookies for us after school, and big mugs of milky tea. But the kitchen hadn't been the same since she died. Neighbors had been bringing us casseroles and cakes, but there wasn't anything waiting on the counter tonight.

Finally, I made us peanut butter toast. There was only enough milk for one glass, so we gave it to Rudy, much as I hated to. It's not that I minded giving him the last of the milk. It's just that he always spills it. That was something else Gabby was working on.

Peanut butter toast probably wasn't what Dad would call

food, but I couldn't see anything else that qualified. I didn't know what he would do if I didn't help him, and I wasn't anxious to find out.

To distract Dad from the toast, I brought him a deck of cards and a big stack of old newspapers to read. They were the kind of newspapers you buy in the grocery store with headlines like GIANT EARTHWORMS EAT ENTIRE KINDERGARTEN CLASS! The story on top of the pile was about a man who had lost eighty pounds eating dog food. "I never felt better!" said the caption underneath a picture of this skinny fellow waving a can opener and a can of dog food.

When I left him, Dad was reading an article about how he could live in Mexico for only fourteen dollars a day.

Upstairs, Christa was complaining that she was still hungry. I told her to wait until Ma got home from work, although we both knew that wouldn't do much good. It had always been Gabby who did the cooking, not Ma.

I looked at the clock. Ma was a few minutes late. I wondered if that meant she was finally doing some Christmas shopping. Every night when she came in, Christa and I looked for packages, bags, or bulges in her coat pocket. There hadn't been any yet, and she was running out of shopping days until Christmas. I reached for the box of toothpicks, shut my eyes, and picked out a few. An even number meant Ma had started her Christmas shopping. An odd number was bad news. I counted them twice just to make sure. Five.

A *whoosh* of cold air around my ankles meant Ma had just

come in the front door. Another *whoosh,* and I knew Peabody had left. When Ma came into the kitchen, I didn't even get excited about the bag under her arm. Five was five, after all. She emptied out two frozen pizzas onto the counter.

"Nick, do you want to fix these?" she asked tiredly, pulling off her coat and heading toward her bedroom.

Frozen pizza! All right! Gabby didn't believe in anything that had to list its ingredients, so everything I knew about frozen food came from the occasional pizza at Tyrone's house.

I suspected that a good first step was to read the directions. Wrong. The first step was to mop up the milk Rudy had spilled on the floor, now that I'd walked through it in my socks.

Reading the directions wasn't that easy, either. My hair kept falling in my eyes. Gabby used to cut my hair. I didn't know who'd do it now, and it was getting pretty shaggy. My grandmother always said I reminded her of a border collie, one of those dogs that can round up a herd of sheep so cleverly that the sheep hardly know what's happening. She said I was good-natured, hardworking, loyal, and just a little bit anxious. How about a whole lot anxious? There was my dad in the basement, Ma shut in her room, Christa and Rudy wanting dinner, and—joy to the world—Christmas was coming.

I read once that border collies like working so much that, if there are no sheep around, they'll start herding the neighbor's cows, the birds in the backyard, or the family cats. Right there you have the difference between me and a border collie. I would have been just as happy to run off and chase a rabbit—*especially* a rabbit—but as it was, my sheep were running all over the hillside and I didn't know how to get them organized again.

Tyrone called while the pizzas were in the oven to say his uncle had just given him all last month's UFO magazines. His uncle is the only person I know, besides Tyrone and me, who is interested in unidentified flying objects. He subscribes to five different magazines, and then he gives them to us after he's read them.

Tyrone and I have been keeping a log of all the UFOs we have sighted. We were just arguing about the last one, which I thought was only a neon light from the Chinese grocery two streets over, when Christa said, "I smell something burning."

I hung up without saying good-bye and got to work scraping the pizzas off the oven rack. When I knocked on Ma's door, her voice sounded muffled. "You kids go ahead and eat without me," she said.

It was strange with just the three of us sitting there. Now that I thought about it, though, I realized Ma hadn't sat down with us at the table since Gabby died. It felt like something was missing. Well, of course, Gabby was missing. And Ma was missing. And Dad hadn't been around in nearly two years. But something else was missing.

"Did you ever hear of plates, Nick? Or napkins?" Christa complained. I realized as she spoke what was missing: plates and napkins.

"We *always* have salad for dinner," continued Christa. "I'm not going to eat until you fix a salad."

I aimed a dirty look where it counted—at Primrose. We all knew who liked salads around here. "If you can find anything to make a salad with," I told Christa, "I'll make one." That was a pretty safe thing to say.

While Christa was busy mopping up Rudy's spilled water after we finished eating, I slid the rest of the pizza onto a napkin and took it down to Dad. I didn't see him at first, and I thought maybe he'd left. Then I was ashamed of myself because I was so happy at the thought.

It's easy to overlook my dad—except when he's mad, of course. It's as though he was colored by some kid who didn't know how to stay inside the lines. His eyes are sort of blurry, and he always needs a shave. His dark, smudgy hair sticks out every which way, and he's so thin his clothes just hang on him. Tyrone's uncle Walter is just the opposite. He is all sharp, straight lines and crisp shirts and sleeked-down hair. His mustache looks painted on, and I think his wife probably parts his hair for him—nobody could get it that even all by himself. When Walter turns sideways, I'm always surprised that he isn't flat, like a paper doll.

Dad was sitting back in the corner by the bikes. He looked up excitedly and said, "Hey, Nick! Listen to this! It says here you can get rich doing absolutely nothing. They guarantee that money will come pouring in while you sleep. And the amazing, secret plan costs only two dollars."

Before I could say anything, he continued quickly, "And it's absolutely legal and honest. All I need is two bucks. Think of it, Nick!"

Before he could ask, I turned my pockets inside out. Empty.

"Right," said my dad, deflating a little against the basement wall. He reached for the pizza and started eating it like it was the amazing, secret plan. I figured it was a good time to find out a few things. My dentist taught me that: You wait until the guy's mouth is full, and then you start asking questions.

"So," I said, "how long do you think you'll be here? I suppose you'll be leaving before Christmas, huh?"

He grunted. "It depends. I've got to call this guy who might have a job for me out West. Of course, with my luck, he was probably run over by a truck yesterday."

I must have looked puzzled because he said, "Well, I mean, all this"—he waved his arms around the dark, cob-webby basement—"it isn't *my* fault I'm here. There's such a thing as bad luck, you know. I've had bad luck all my life. My old man was drunk most of the time, and I inherited the drinking from him."

He finished the last of the pizza and said, "I could have done real well in school, but the teachers were always down on me, probably because of my old man. I thought things were going to change with your ma, but I needed somebody who could understand me and look up to me—you know, make me feel good. But she's a narrow-minded woman, your ma is. Then I got in with some guys that . . . Well, when they offered me a job, I thought maybe my luck was going to change. And it should have. Nobody could touch me when it came to selling cars. But they told me that there wasn't anything wrong with turning the odometer back."

"Odometer? What's that?" I said. I had to get this part straight because I didn't know why my dad got sent to prison. Ma and Gabby would never talk about it.

"You know those numbers on the dashboard that tell you how many miles you've got on your car?" he asked.

"Yeah," I said. "One of Tyrone's grandmas has a car with 125,000 miles on it. That must be some kind of record, huh?"

"Aw, that's nothing," he said. "The car that did me in had 175,000 miles on it before I turned it back."

"What do you mean, 'turned it back'?" I said.

He explained that it's easier to sell a car that hasn't got a lot of miles on it, so the auto dealership he worked for used to turn cars' odometers back if they had too many miles on them.

"Like, see, we'd get a car with 100,000 miles on it, and we'd turn it back to 35,000 miles. I didn't know that was against the law. I was just following orders. But the judge wasn't buying that, no sir. See what I mean? What kind of luck is that?"

I tried to feel sorry for my dad, seeing as how he had had such rotten luck all his life, but I couldn't help thinking that, when *I* had talked like that, Gabby had called it whining.

Maybe for a minute there I didn't look too sympathetic, because he gave me a narrow look and said, "You're not thinking for yourself again, are you? Anybody who believes in creatures from outer space does not play with a full deck. You let me do the thinking around here."

I winced. My dad always used to make fun of my interest in UFOs. I had hoped he'd forgotten about it.

"It might have crossed your mind that you could turn me in to the cops. Don't do it," he said. "Your ma would probably . . ."

Ma! I'd almost forgotten what it would do to Ma if she knew Dad was down here. Just thinking of the two of them in the same breath stirred up all kinds of memories. Some of them were happy memories: Dad and Ma cuddling on the sofa. Ma winning hand after hand when Dad taught her how to play gin rummy. The two of them sitting down to gourmet dinners that Dad had spent all afternoon fixing. Rudy wasn't born then, but Christa and I used to sneak out of our bedrooms and peek around the corner at them as they ate by candlelight. They didn't seem to care that they were sitting on chairs that didn't match and eating at a wobbly old card table.

Unfortunately, most of my memories were of Ma crying—crying while she walked me to kindergarten, crying while she changed Christa's diaper (nothing makes Christa madder than to remind her that I knew her when she was in diapers), crying while she told Christa and me we were going to have a new baby brother or sister, crying while we drove back across the state to Gabby's—without Dad. She still cried after we moved in with Gabby. Once she said to me, "You must be pretty sick of the tears, Nick. But I'll tell you what"—she smiled a damp, wavery smile—"I think I'm about finished. I think what you're seeing here are the last of the Monty tears."

I sure hoped never to see any more Monty tears. The last thing Ma needed now on top of Gabby dying was to run into the one guy in the whole world guaranteed to make her cry.

Right then and there, I made one of those lightning decisions for which I am *not* famous. I decided I was going to do every little thing my dad wanted, just the way he wanted it, and twice as fast as he wanted it. It was like the old joke: Where does an eight-hundred-pound gorilla sit? (Answer: anywhere he wants to.)

When I went back upstairs, I was surprised to see that the kitchen looked exactly the way it had half an hour before. Pizza crusts and wrinkled napkins lay where we had dropped them. Gabby would have had the whole kitchen cleaned in fifteen minutes. We used to say she could catch a dirty sock before it hit the floor. Who was going to take care of everything now that Gabby was gone?

I looked around, but there was only me. The house was so quiet I could hear the clock in the other room. Christa and Rudy must have been in their bedroom, and I suppose Ma was in hers. Before Gabby died, there would have been the clank of silverware and the clatter of plates as Gabby did dishes. Rudy and Christa would have been shrieking and chasing around in some silly game of their own. And Ma would have been watching the news. But now it was so quiet my ears hurt.

After putting the dishes in the sink to soak, I took out the box of toothpicks. An even number meant Ma would let us get started with the Christmas baking and decorating. I concentrated hard on not cheating as I reached in the box. I looked. Six!

When I knocked on Ma's door, she didn't answer at first and I thought she must be sleeping. But then I heard a faint "Come in." She was lying on her bed, staring at the ceiling. She was holding Gabby's funeral handkerchief. When I saw that, I knew she must be feeling really bad, so I started to back out.

She fingered it and said, "Did I ever tell you about this handkerchief?"

"No," I said, "but Gabby said that . . ."

Ma didn't hear me. She smoothed the soft flowery cotton and straightened the lace edges. It was very soft lace, not the kind that scratches your nose. I know, because Gabby let me touch it.

"Gabby carried this handkerchief when my little brother died. She carried it to my dad's funeral. And to her best friend Anna's funeral. It's never been washed, so it still has her tears on it."

I didn't know what to say. Whenever I tried talking about Gabby, Ma would either stare blankly at me and get up and leave, or she'd say, "Not now, Nicky, okay?"

I waited to see if she was going to say anything else, but after I stood there a few minutes, I cleared my throat—sort of to change the subject—and said, "Look, Ma, it's only four more days until Christmas, and we haven't even started to get ready. Could I get out the tree tonight, or could we bake some cookies or something?"

In spite of the toothpicks, I knew what she was going to say before she said it. "Tomorrow" had always been her favorite word, even when Gabby was alive. Now it seemed to be her only word. She kept saying she'd feel better tomorrow, that she'd get it together tomorrow. If we could just give her a little time . . .

"Nick, I really will get started. I've been thinking about Christmas. I just haven't been able to face it yet. But tomorrow . . . maybe after work I'll pick up some groceries and we'll bake cookies after dinner and put up the tree while they're baking and . . . Okay, Nicky? It's just that it was always Gabby who . . ." She rolled over and started crying again. I left, shutting the door very, very gently, the way you do when you really want to slam it.

Yes, I was sorry for her, and sorry about Gabby, and sorry for everybody in the whole world. And I felt guilty for wanting a tree and presents and cookies and all the rest of it. But I still wanted Christmas to be the way it had always been. I stomped through the living room, seeing for the first time how shabby and bare our house was. Had it always been like this, or had it seemed different when Gabby was alive? The only really nice thing in the living room was the music box. I stopped to look at it and realized that we would never know its secret now that Gabby had died.

When Gabby was a baby, she had been left in the entryway of an orphanage—just Gabby, the basket she lay in, a hand-knitted red-and-green blanket, and the strange, beautiful music box. Gabby spent the first half of her life trying to find out who her family was and why she had been left at the orphanage. The music box was the only clue she had. But it turned out to be no help at all.

I could never understand why Gabby gave up looking, but she told me once that all the searching and wondering kept her from getting on with her life. She had wasted the first half of it wishing for the impossible. So she made up her mind to spend the last half being happy. But she treasured the music box anyway. She said it was all the family she had. It was family to me, too. I wanted that music box to play.

I went back in the kitchen and looked at the toothpicks on the shelf. There were still six of them. I must have dropped one on the floor without noticing.

When the phone rang, I jumped about a foot. Nothing wrong with my nerves, right? It was some man for Ma, which was odd since I didn't think she knew any. After I called her, I stood very still and tried to look like part of the wallpaper so she wouldn't notice me listening.

"Yes. . . . No. . . . Yes, of course. I'll let you know right away if he tries to contact us. . . . Thank you."

Ma hung up, turned around stiffly, saw me, and said, "You probably should know this, too, Nick. Your father has left the minimum-security facility where he was finishing his term. He didn't report in last night when he should have. They thought we should know about it."

You probably have to have a college education to be a criminal today so you can understand words like "odometer" and "minimum-security facility." Ma explained that it's a place where the prisoners work at ordinary jobs as long as they return to the prison every night.

"Be sure to keep the doors locked, and don't let anybody in before you check to see who it is," she said.

I just about choked. It was too late for locked doors at our house.

Ma isn't usually very good with straight answers, but I thought tonight might be different because she seemed upset by the phone call. "Ma, what would you do if Dad came to the door? Are you afraid of him? What's he really like? I remember some bad times from before, but sometimes I'm not sure if they all really happened or if I dreamed some of them."

She was quiet for so long I thought she wasn't going to answer me. But then she said, "Come here. I want to show you something."

I followed her into her bedroom, where she pulled a photograph in a fancy frame from under her bed. It showed a handsome, smiling man I could just barely recognize as my dad.

"This is the man I married. In a way, this is your real father. But, in another way, the man who broke the law, and the man who was . . . well, I can't make it easier for you, Nick. You're old enough to know that your dad drank too much and was often violent. You remember some of that. Anyway, that was your real father, too. I wanted to help him, but I couldn't, because he didn't think he had a problem. He was the only person who could save himself, but he never figured that out."

"Why is he—I mean, why was he like that?" I said.

"We all have some good in us and some bad in us, Nick. But your dad—well, he didn't try to use the good part of him to work on the bad part. All his life he blamed other people for his troubles, so of course he wasn't about to try to change himself when it wasn't *his* fault."

I couldn't believe she was actually talking to me about

my dad. I had a million questions saved up from the last couple of years. "Why did you marry Dad if he was like that? And how can people love somebody and not love them at the same time? Did Dad always make you cry? I remember you guys laughing a lot, too. Wasn't that enough? Why didn't you go see a marriage counselor or something?"

But Ma has only so much talk in her, and I could see she was fresh out. I remember one time Gabby said Ma was "sensitive." It was the artistic temperament, according to Gabby, and we had to make allowances for it. Christa said she didn't think it was fair that Ma got an allowance and we didn't. Christa is so dumb sometimes.

Anyway, I don't think Ma even heard my questions about Dad. She slid the picture back under the bed and, when she turned around, she seemed surprised to see I was still there. I sighed and let her kiss me good-night. I know when I've dropped my bucket into an empty well.

I lay awake most of the night, worrying about what my dad might do next. Even in my room with the door closed, I couldn't shut out the picture of him down there in the basement. And there was the furry, frightening thought that crawled all over me in the dark: Was I going to turn out like my dad? Was his bad luck going to be passed on to me, just like he got his from his dad? More than anything in the world, I didn't want to be like my dad.

I made myself think about something else. Christmas. Maybe somebody else would believe his mother when she said she'd get going tomorrow. But I had had a lot of experience with Ma. She meant well, she really did. But tomorrow never came for her. It was always Gabby who took us to the dentist, signed our field-trip permission slips, and made birthday cakes.

I could see Ma huddled on her bed, crying like a little kid. That was the problem. Somebody had always taken care of Ma. Who would take care of her now? I was afraid I might get the job, and I didn't want it. I was just a kid myself.

That's not to say Ma wasn't a good mother. Actually, Tyrone wishes he had one like her. If Gabby took care of all the practical things, Ma was the one who made things fun—or at least she did before Gabby died.

One night last summer, she drove Tyrone and me out into the country to watch for UFOs. We parked on a gravel road where the countryside was flat for miles around and the skies were heavy with stars and who knows what else. The three of us sat on the warm hood of the car, waiting for a UFO to appear. We ate a three-pound bag of apples between us. And, no, we didn't spot any UFOs, but it was still fun. Another time, she spent a whole day helping us build an igloo out of snow blocks. She's probably read us about a million books since we were born, and I was always tripping over her playing pig pile with Christa and Rudy in the middle of the living room floor.

Ma doesn't seem to actually do much of anything, but

everybody feels better when she's around. She works at a florist shop, and she's always bringing home sick plants. She doesn't seem to do much for them, either, but they just go crazy for her. Even now, I don't particularly want her to do anything for us—although dinner would be nice. I just wish she'd be with us again like she used to. She's here, but she's not here, if that makes sense.

So there I was, as desperate for all the trappings of Christmas as any three-year-old. But Gabby, who'd always made Christmas happen, wasn't there anymore; my mother was about as helpful as one of her ferns; and my dad wasn't much better. If Christmas was ever going to come to our house, it was up to me. Good old border collie Nick was going to organize those sheep.

 ## *December 21*

The next morning was the last day of school before Christmas. In art class we finished the sun catchers we were making for Christmas presents. Everybody else was using the forms the teacher handed out to make rainbows, birds, or sunsets. But I was making something special—a whole stack of two-inch-square designs that looked like stained-glass windows. In fact, they looked a lot like stained-glass windows. Tiny ones. Tyrone was the only one who knew what they were for.

When I walked in the house from school, Rudy attached himself to my leg, so I dragged him along, left-riiiiight, left-riiiiight, to the kitchen for a snack.

At first I thought Gabby must have come back. The breakfast dishes were done and put away, the floor was swept, and the counters were all cleared off. Then I remembered that Dad had been alone in the house all day today, probably bored out of his mind, and that he used to help Gabby clear up after dinner if he was in a good mood. It was great to have the kitchen done, but I hoped that he'd remembered to make those phone calls about a job, too.

I didn't notice Christa was in the kitchen until I heard this disgusting *squish, squish* noise. Did you ever watch a rabbit eat peanut butter? I don't recommend it. I ate my toast in the other room so I wouldn't have to listen. I pulled last month's *Cosmic Search* out of my back pocket and set it on the mantel. Normally I'd be dying to get at it, but today I had other things on my mind.

First I cleaned up the milk I had just dragged Rudy through (left-riiiiight, left-riiiiight) and then dressed him. I thought of waking Peabody to help out, but it didn't seem worth the trouble.

I took a loaf of bread, a jar of peanut butter, and a can of warm beer that I found in the back of the cupboard down to Dad. He was extremely polite and even thanked me several times. I figured he was either very hungry or going crazy. As it turned out, he was neither.

I wanted to get started on the Christmas decorations, but the boxes were stored above the basement ceiling beams, and I couldn't get them down by myself. I was really surprised that as soon as I mentioned the problem to Dad, he jumped up and zipped over to get them. He wasn't usually so helpful. While he was getting them down, I happened to glance at the newspaper he had been reading. The headline said, UNHAPPY TEENAGE BOY TURNS INTO WEREWOLF AND ATTACKS PARENTS.

When I thanked Dad for carrying the boxes to the top of the stairs, I couldn't help experimenting with a fangy sort of smile.

There was still a nail on our front door from last year, so the first thing I did was to Frisbee the green-and-red plastic wreath up onto it. The first sign of Christmas!

Tyrone was just coming up the walk. It reminded me of how I met him. He had been coming up my walk then, too. The only difference was that he was running and breathing fire that time, while I was hiding behind a bush and trying to keep my knees from knocking.

Tyrone was this big guy—I mean, he had teeth the size of dominoes, and he had to wear a rope for a belt. He was king of the neighborhood, and I had heard that if he didn't like you, he could turn your whole body into a pretzel.

One day at school, I was talking to some kids and I made this perfectly innocent remark about how much food it must take to feed a guy like Tyrone. He overheard me, and I guess he misunderstood my scientific interest in caloric intake related to body size. He decided to rearrange my face. And I knew from the way he said it that he would do it in the most painful way possible. No anesthesia for *this* patient!

So there I was, behind a bush that had lost most of its leaves, and there was Tyrone, a guy with a mission. And pretty good eyesight to boot.

He had one hand wrapped twice around my neck, and the other in a fist (probably no bigger than a basketball) aimed at my nose when I was visited by inspiration.

"Oh, my gawrsh!" I gargled as best I could. "There's a UFO!" And I pointed a shaky hand skyward.

Well, talk about magic! Tyrone let go so suddenly I bounced twice on the pavement. He whipped a little notebook and stubby pencil out of his back pocket, checked his watch quickly, and wrote the time down at the top of a fresh page. "Now, where was it, what did it look like, and which direction was it going?" he asked.

I sat down beside him, pulled out *my* little notebook, and started making up a sighting as fast as I could. (Later, after we became *very* good friends, I told him he might as well rip out that page.)

Tyrone's been my best friend ever since, and I hardly ever hear anyone call him a bully anymore.

Tyrone followed me into the house. Stepping over Peabody's legs, he said, "Does your ma actually pay this zombie? I wouldn't mind work like that. Talk to your ma about it, will you?"

Actually, I would have liked to talk to Ma about Peabody, but I didn't think she could handle trying to find another baby-sitter. I figured everything had been okay so far, and I'd just keep my fingers crossed.

Tyrone pulled two chairs together, sat down, and started to read to me from one of the UFO magazines—a really good article called "Aliens Crash Birthday Party in Bangor, Maine"—while I set out the red and green candles, trying to remember the way Gabby had them last year. When I found the four carved wooden letters that spelled NOEL, Tyrone jumped up and said to let him do it. He carefully arranged them on the mantel next to the music box. While he did that, I dressed Rudy again.

Tyrone backed into Christa. "Tell me the truth, Christa," he said. "Do you come up and stand behind people so they'll trip over you?"

Christa set Primrose down on the floor, pointed to Tyrone, and said, "Go get him, Primrose!"

Tyrone bleated furiously, jumped up on the sofa, and began flapping his arms like someone who has just seen Bigfoot coming out of the woods. Once Christa had read Tyrone a paragraph from a book on rabbits, about what they can do with their little razor teeth. According to Christa, rabbits are right up there with beavers in the tooth department. Another time, Christa showed Tyrone pictures of a cute little bunny and the sofa it ate. In the first picture, the sofa looked like an average pretty nice yellow-and-green sofa with just a few rabbit toothmarks along the bottom. But in the later pictures, you could watch the sofa disappear before your eyes. That rabbit ate the padded arms, the upholstery, the pillows, and even the wooden frame. After that, Tyrone never seemed very relaxed at our house.

I wasn't surprised when he remembered he had to get home right away. I put Christa and Primrose to work unpacking the box of tree ornaments so Tyrone could get down from the sofa. But somewhere between there and the front door, Rudy barnacled onto Tyrone's right leg. Tyrone was wearing the same kind of jeans I was, so it was an easy mistake to make. I thought he peeled Rudy off his leg a little roughly, and I hope he wasn't talking about us when he left muttering, "Bughouse, absolute bughouse." It wasn't as if I couldn't find another best friend if I had to.

By the time I returned from seeing Tyrone off, Christa had unpacked all the ornaments and was holding the last one in her hand—a shiny red glass ball. "I think we used to have more of these," she said slowly. "I had a dream once. I was really little, and we were decorating the Christmas tree. A man came in, and I don't know why, but he started yelling. Then there was *snick! snick! snick!* on the wood floor, and suddenly broken red glass was everywhere."

I didn't say anything to Christa, but that was no dream. I suppose it was easier for her to think of it that way. But I was a little surprised that she didn't recognize the guy in her "dream."

I started sorting the ornaments, setting aside the ones that were missing their little wire hangers.

"Christa, do you remember Dad?" I asked.

She looked at me indignantly, hands on hips, and said, "Of course I remember my own father! What do you think, I'm crazy or something? Just because we don't talk about him around here doesn't mean I've forgotten him."

Then she frowned and said cautiously, "Well, I don't remember a *lot*. I mean, I was only six when he left, and I don't think he was around very much even before that. Was he?"

I shook my head, and said, "What *do* you remember?"

She stretched out on her stomach on the floor, propped her head up on her hands, and said slowly, "When I can't get to sleep at night, I think about how Daddy used to scoop me up and sit me on his lap while he read the paper. Every once in a while, he'd give me a hug, although I think his mind was mostly on the paper. But afterward, if I had been very still and hadn't interrupted him, he'd throw down the paper, turn to me, and say, 'My little sweetheart. My really fine Christa.' And he'd look at me and tuck my hair behind my ears and hug me again."

She turned to me sharply and said, "Don't say anything. I know he wasn't the greatest. I haven't forgotten some of the . . . well, I know he wasn't perfect. But he loved me a lot. Almost every night I fall asleep thinking of how he used to say, 'My little sweetheart. My really fine Christa.' "

That was one of the longest speeches Christa had ever made. I didn't know what to say. So I plugged in a string of Christmas tree lights and started looking for burned-out ones.

The wreath on the door, the candles, and the NOEL on the mantel—all that little stuff was just a warm-up. Now it was time to get to the main event—putting up the aluminum Christmas tree. The directions had been lost years before, so I had to do it "by guess and by golly," as Gabby used to say. All the while I was working, I was imagining Ma coming home from work, seeing the tree, and smiling. This would put her in the old Christmas spirit, for sure.

It was a good thing I had something to look forward to, because I spent nearly two hours engaged in mortal combat with that tree. The good news is that, although I got pretty beat up, I managed to assemble the monster. The bad news is that the tree looked worse than I did.

I was just draping the last of the tinsel on the tree when I felt eyes watching me. You know that creepy feeling? There was nobody behind me, nobody to the right, and nobody to the left. That meant . . . Christa and Primrose were gazing steadily at me from the corner behind the Christmas tree.

"Christa, how did you get in there?" I yelled.

"You didn't even notice me," she complained. "Here I am just standing in the corner minding my own business, and you come along and put up a Christmas tree in my face."

I thought of several things to say, beginning with "Can't you *talk?*" and ending with remarks that would have gotten me sent to my room for a very long time.

I had to practically take the tree down again to get them out. Primrose had tried to chew on the aluminum "bark" and was spitting daintily and giving me dirty looks. As if it were my fault we have an aluminum tree, for crying out loud. By the time I got them out of there and fixed the tree again, I was so mad I almost had smoke coming out of my ears. Christa backed away from me and whispered, "Birdhouse, Nick! Birdhouse."

She was right. I dropped my screwdriver right there and walked very carefully through the kitchen, down the basement stairs, and over to my workbench. Dad looked up from the solitaire game spread out in front of him and said, "Pretty rough up there, eh? I know! I know! Don't talk to you, right?"

Everybody knew that when things were really getting to me, the best way to head off World War III was for me to go to the basement and build birdhouses until I felt better.

The birdhouse I was working on was almost finished, but a little extra sanding never hurt anything, so I sanded back and forth, back and forth, along the edges, paying particular attention to the little dowel that served as a perch. My breathing got slower and slower, and first thing you know I was humming "O Christmas Tree." I went over the birdhouse one last time and then set it on the shelf with all the others. I was ready to go back upstairs.

But first I had to ask my dad a question. I went over and watched him play solitaire. If the four of hearts didn't turn up pretty soon, he was going to lose. And my dad didn't like losing at solitaire. He gently riffled the edges of the cards in his hand until he spotted the four of hearts, and then, with a flick of his fingers, he slipped it onto the top of the deck.

"Dad, why did you leave that, uh, place?"

"Well, I didn't mean to, that's for sure!" he said, slapping down the four of hearts on the hearts pile.

"You didn't mean to?" I stood there, trying to figure out how you could escape from prison without meaning to.

"Well, here's the thing," he said. "I was walking to the auto body shop one morning—" He interrupted himself to explain, "They let me work there every day, but I had to go back to the joint at night. Anyway, my buddy and I were walking past Fleeson's Department Store, and there was this guy out front taping up a sign that said WANTED: SANTA CLAUS."

I got the feeling that this might be a long story, so I sat down, picked up the other deck of cards, and started laying them out for solitaire.

Dad reached over to straighten one of my piles and continued, "This guy told us that they'd been advertising a visit from Santa Claus for weeks. This was the big day, but the fellow who was supposed to do the Claus number was sick. Then he started grumbling about how you'd have to be pretty sick to give up fifty dollars for such an easy day's work. I couldn't believe it! Fifty big ones for sitting around in a red suit all day! So I told my buddy to cover for me at the shop, and I went right in to ask for the job. I figured that was the easiest money I'd ever make."

He sighed and added darkly, "What I didn't know at the time was that it was danger money." Dad stopped for a minute, evidently lost in unpleasant thoughts.

"You have no idea," he said at last. "They stuffed me with pillows and strapped me into a thick, itchy suit and glued whiskers on my face. They had to practically carry me to the chair, and once they put me in it, I couldn't get enough leverage to get out again. Did you ever read that story about a guy who got turned into a great big beetle and he was just lying there on his back with his legs waving in the air and he couldn't get up?"

I shook my head no.

"Well, anyway, that's what I felt like. But that wasn't the half of it," he went on. "No sir, the suit wasn't the half of it. Then came the kids." His voice began to rise.

"They stepped on my feet, they pulled my beard, they poked my stomach. They coughed in my face, they wiped their noses on my sleeve, and they spit when they talked. Some of them were kind of cute until they smiled, and then—ugh!—they were missing their little front teeth. They *all* had sticky hands. Some of them were carrying damp little half-eaten lollipops, and one little kid must have been eating jelly with his hands. Then there were the ones who took one look at me and started shrieking. The parents weren't any better. When I told one kid to shut up, his dad offered to make me eat my beard."

Dad looked at the cards in front of him, but I don't think he really saw them. He said glumly, "And then they wouldn't let me go at five o'clock. I was supposed to report back by five-thirty, but the store was open until nine, and they said I had to stay. They actually got very unpleasant when I tried to sneak out."

I said, "Well, at least you got all that money."

I wouldn't have thought it was possible, but his face got even glummer.

"Yeah, well, actually I didn't," he said. "You have to understand that after a whole day with those little . . . those little, ah, *children*, my nerves were totally shot. And you know how some little kids sort of slobber? Well, this one little kid came along and he kissed me right on the lips. And he was *real* slobbery. I lost it, you know? I just had no control. Before I knew what was happening, I was on my feet, running down the up escalator and out through the big front doors."

Dad sighed and scooped up his cards. He shuffled them halfheartedly and said, "So there I was, free as a jaybird just when I wasn't expecting it."

"I think the expression is 'naked as a jaybird,' Dad," I said.

He glared at me, and said, "I was not! In fact, it wasn't until a police officer said, 'Merry Christmas, Mr. Claus!' that

I realized I was still dressed in the Santa suit. But what a great disguise! Then it dawned on me. I had already been reported missing, so I might as well just stay on the outside. A couple of guys had talked about jobs once I got out, and I thought if I could get work in another state, nobody'd ever find me. But in the meantime, I had to make a few calls and lie low until I got things arranged. So here I am."

Dad was working on a new game of solitaire by now, and he needed a jack of diamonds. I found the jack of diamonds from my deck and handed it to him. He just slapped it right down and kept on playing. Strange guy, my dad. He didn't much care how he got where he was going. Just so he got there.

I left him still slapping those cards down. Upstairs, Christa and Rudy had plugged in the tree lights and were sitting in front of it. Rudy was absentmindedly pulling off his socks, and Primrose was pushing an ornament around on the floor with her nose.

Peabody suddenly sat up, pointed to the mantel, and said, "Who's Leon? Which one of you kids is Leon?"

"Christa, you quit it!" I said. I quickly rearranged the letters to spell NOEL.

 ## *December 21*

*(CONTINUED)*

I tried not to be disappointed. Ma works hard at the florist shop, and I suppose she was tired. It was just that I had wanted her to be happy when she saw the Christmas tree. I thought it would cheer her up. Instead, when she came in the living room, her face crumpled and she went in her bedroom and shut the door. I guess I just made things worse.

When she finally came out, she sent Peabody home and then sat holding the mail and looking out the window. Christa and Rudy started to fight about something, and Ma just looked at them. Right away, they both got very quiet. Actually, I was surprised Ma even heard them because she seemed to be in another world most of the time.

I asked her when we were eating dinner and what we were having. Christa and Rudy and I were hungry, and I thought it would be nice if we could talk about dinner. She didn't eat anymore herself, and it got so that I felt guilty if she saw me chowing down—as if I didn't love Gabby very much if I could still eat.

She said, "Dinner? Oh, dinner. Well, I suppose we could . . . I don't know, open a can of . . . of . . ."

"I could fix something," I offered.

"Mmm," she said, and I knew I had lost her.

"Like spaghetti or grilled cheese sandwiches." These were Tyrone's specialties, and I figured I could call him up so he could walk me through them.

"Yes, well . . ." she said.

I couldn't resist.

"On the other hand," I said, "maybe I'll just fry up a couple of those nice brown paper grocery bags with the handles."

"Well, whatever, Nick . . ."

See what I mean?

I got out the can opener and pulled out cans of chili and fruit cocktail. That was one nice thing, anyway—Ma had finally gone grocery shopping. When you learn grocery shopping, you must start with cans because that's all she brought home. Maybe next week she will learn about boxes and then go on to things like fruits and vegetables.

When the doorbell rang, Ma was in her room again, and

I wasn't too sure I should open the door at night. The porch light had burned out, and Ma hadn't gotten around to replacing it.

But it was just a friend of Gabby's bringing us a Christmas fruitcake. You couldn't pay me to eat fruitcake—I think it looks like fancy dog food—but it came in a red-and-green Christmas tin that looked cheerful, so I took it.

I was interested to meet one of Gabby's friends. She used to talk about them a lot—Sylvia, Albertine, and Ruth—but I never saw them because they only came to visit when I was in school. From what I could figure out, they mainly drank tea and moved furniture.

I used to come home from school and think I'd walked into the wrong house. The TV would be missing. The sofa would appear in somebody's bedroom. The entire dining room would be moved to a corner of the living room. And Primrose would be hiding—she hated furniture-moving days.

Gabby used to buy old rolls of wallpaper at rummage sales, and there was never enough to do the whole room, so she would just paper half a wall or maybe the ceiling or maybe two walls with one kind of paper and two walls with another kind. If an alien ever does come to visit (I once signed up to be a host), I'm going to have a hard time explaining our house.

Sylvia-Albertine-Ruth told me that one of the last things she and Gabby ever talked about was me. Gabby told her

I really had my head screwed on right. That meant a lot to me because I don't think anybody in his whole life ever said my dad's head was screwed on right. Maybe I wasn't as much like him as I thought.

Which reminded me of him. Before I went to bed, I sneaked downstairs to see if he needed anything else. He was hiding, but when I whispered, "Dad!" he came out and said, "Oh, it's you."

"Who did you think it was? I'm the only one who ever comes down here," I said.

I was shocked when he said, "I thought Gabby might come down for something."

He didn't know.

When I told him Gabby was dead, he just stared at me with this kind of goofy look. It was the same look I got when he said crazy things like how he was going to hide out in the basement for a while. I knew how he felt. The words "Gabby" and "dead" just didn't seem to go together. She was the most alive person you could imagine, and she was always there. It would be like coming out to the kitchen in the morning and finding a big empty space where the stove used to be. You'd say, "What!" and you'd scratch your head and you wouldn't believe what your eyes were seeing.

After staring at the cement floor for a while, he shook his head sadly and said, "That is one darn shame. That is . . . that is just one darn shame. I really liked Gabby. She always treated me the same, no matter what happened. I was no saint, of course . . ." He looked up sharply at me, but I didn't say anything. He usually liked me to agree with him. In this case, I thought I'd just pass.

". . . but Gabby was really decent to me. And, by golly, could that woman play cards! She wasn't supposed to, you know. She'd been raised real strict in the orphanage—card playing was a sin and all that. But she made some deal with God. I don't know what it was. But she'd worked out something where she could play cards."

He scuffled his foot a little, and then said almost shyly, "Gabby used to like me. In the beginning. I was sorry about that. I mean, that it had to change. She was glad when your ma left me."

He looked at me for a minute and said, "You know, I always thought you were a lot like Gabby." I was kind of embarrassed at the way my dad was looking at me. And then, too, that was one of the nicest things he ever said to me.

"Gabby was a good woman," he said finally, and I knew that he wasn't going to say any more about her.

To change the subject, I pointed to his shirt pocket and said, "Got any new card tricks?"

"Do chickens have beaks?" he said, with a laugh. "Of course I do! Look here. What do you see?" Quick as anything, he riffled the whole deck in front of my eyes.

"Well," I said, "I see a normal deck of cards. Why? What's wrong with it?"

"Nothing at all!" he said, tapping the deck sharply against the wall. "But look at it now."

Once again he riffled the deck right in front of me. Every last card in the deck was a five of spades!

"What? Huh? How'd you do that?" I couldn't get over it. I was watching every move, and there was no way he did anything to those cards.

"That's for me to know and for you to find out!" he said smugly. "Now you better get back on upstairs."

As I left, I could hear the *slap, slap* of shuffling cards, and I knew he was settling down to another marathon solitaire game. It was his dream to go to Las Vegas someday and beat the bank at solitaire.

In bed that night, I thought about what my dad had said, that I was like Gabby. Wouldn't it be great if I was? I often tried to imagine what would happen if a UFO landed in our backyard. Of course I would invite the aliens to stay with us for a while to learn about our civilization. I always pictured them sitting neatly at the kitchen table watching all of us, maybe taking notes and talking among themselves.

I thought Gabby would be easy for them to understand. She was always the same—busy, cheerful, humming a little, smiling a lot. She was her own person. She did what she had to do, no matter what anybody else was doing. I thought the aliens would like her and feel comfortable with her.

Ma and Dad now, that was another story. Although they were very different from each other, they were alike in some ways, too. What would the aliens make of Dad's moods and his yelling? If *we* couldn't figure him out half the time, how could they? And what would they make of Ma's worrying and handwringing?

So when I think about taking after Gabby or taking after Ma and Dad, I always look at it from the aliens' point of view and decide I'd rather be like Gabby. At least you knew what Gabby was all about. Ma and Dad were too confusing, and I didn't want to live my whole life trying to figure myself out.

Besides, Ma and Dad both needed keepers. I didn't want to be like that, either—always waiting for other people to fix things for me. Nobody had ever had to take care of Gabby. She was strong. On the other hand, what was the good of being strong when it meant you spent your whole life taking care of other people? Did it have to be one way or the other? Did you have to either take care of people or be taken care of? Couldn't you just sort of take care of yourself?

I was falling asleep on that idea when Dad came barreling in my door and dove under my bed. Seconds later, Ma came in.

"Nick?" she said. "Was that you in the hall?"

"Yes, no," I said. I figured that would cover it.

"Well, you get to sleep. It's too late to be prowling around."

"It sure is!" I said through my teeth after she left.

Dad hitched himself out from under my bed. Being Dad, he didn't apologize, but he said, "I thought everybody would be asleep by now. How would you like to be cooped up in a basement for days at a time?"

I didn't say it, but I couldn't help thinking that it was his choice to be down there.

"Anyway, I won't be staying here much longer," he said. "I'm waiting to hear from this guy down in Florida. He's got a job for me."

After he left, I remembered that the last time, he said it was "some guy out West." His plans didn't sound very solid. How much longer would things go on this way?

If my dad had come into the house and said to himself, "I'm going to make that boy's life a misery," he couldn't have done a better job of it. I wondered if I was too young for an ulcer.

# CHAPTER FIVE

# ❄ *December 22*

It was the first day of Christmas vacation, and I woke up while it was still dark out. I lay there for a while, thinking of all the things I had to do. When I heard Ma getting up for work, I pulled on jeans and my sweatshirt that read REAL MEN EAT CONCRETE and went out to the kitchen to make her a cup of coffee. She didn't know which way was up in the morning until she'd had her coffee, although lately she seemed to be outgrowing it. The last couple of times I made her coffee, I noticed she hardly drank any of it.

"Good morning, Nick!" she said softly. "Oh, say, you don't have to make me coffee. No, really, please, just . . . I'll . . . Oh, well, sure, go ahead if you want to." She sighed. See what I mean? She can hardly function without that coffee.

I knew she had to leave for work in a few minutes, so I didn't have much time to get to the subject of Christmas. I went for the first thing I could think of.

"Was Christmas pretty important to you when you were a kid, Ma?"

She brushed her flyaway reddish hair off her face and didn't seem to notice that it flopped right back. "Yes, yes, it was," she said, and she trailed out of the kitchen.

So much for getting her on the subject of Christmas.

As soon as she left for work, I took Dad some breakfast. I asked him nicely to quit the prowling around because I didn't want to get on Ma's bad side, what with Christmas coming and all. He said he had just wanted to see Christa and Rudy, so he sneaked into their room when he thought everybody was in bed.

"And it's a heck of a thing," he said, "to have one of your own kids bite you."

"Bite you?"

"Before I could even turn the flashlight on, one of 'em jumped out of bed and bit me on the ankle. The other two didn't even wake up," he said.

"Other two?" I said weakly.

"What's the matter with you?" he said. "And, say, I thought your ma and I had only three kids. This kid that bit me— he's no kid of mine!"

"No, no," I said, "that was Primrose."

"Primrose!" he said. "That's a heck of a name for a kid. For *sure* that one isn't mine."

When I explained about Primrose, he seemed almost disappointed. I think he liked the idea of having a real aggressive kid.

The first thing on my Christmas list that day was sugarplums. Gabby had made them every Christmas that I could remember. It seemed to me that they weren't very hard to make. But then, when Gabby made them, I used to spend the whole time leaning on the counter and licking spoons, which is not good training for making sugarplums.

In fact, I really don't want to talk about the whole thing, except to say that I found out that the house *could* burn down and Peabody might not wake up. At one point, I had to open the back door because the kitchen was filled with smoke and Christa and Rudy were crying.

Primrose lay on her back on the kitchen floor with her legs in the air. "Very funny, Primrose," I said. I was about to wake Peabody when Mrs. Morrison from next door came to see where all the smoke was coming from. She had never made sugarplums, but she understood baking so she helped me finish them.

Christa and Rudy watched a Christmas special on TV while I cleaned up the kitchen. The sugarplums looked almost as nice as Gabby's. And the kitchen smelled like dates and orange rind and frosting—and a little bit like smoke.

Outside, the sun was bouncing brilliantly off the snow. And I could hear "Jingle Bells" coming from the TV.

So why wasn't I happy?

Part of it was the fact that Gabby wasn't there. But most of it was that Dad *was*. I could feel him down there, irritable and unpredictable. I always thought you automatically loved your parents unless they were monsters, in which case you automatically hated them. But it wasn't so easy with Dad.

I once read a story in one of Dad's newspapers about a four-year-old girl who got lost in the woods and was saved by a bear. Now bear in mind (pardon the pun) that this story came from a newspaper not particularly known for checking its facts. But it seems that the bear came across this little girl crying in the woods, and it brought her berries and dried meat and kept her warm at night by sleeping next to her. The people who found the little girl many days later said she would certainly have died if the bear hadn't taken care of her.

I think this story is a good way to explain how I feel about my dad. Imagine, for a moment, that I am the bear and my dad is the little girl. No, no, I'm kidding. Of *course* my dad is the bear. I love him for keeping me warm and bringing me food, and like any normal kid, I'm crazy about this big old lovable furry bear. But, I ask you, do you think I would actually shut my eyes and sleep at night? A four-year-old might do that. Me, Nick, who has read many bear books—and who has had some experience with this particular bear—do you really think I would sleep well at night?

"Nick!" called Christa. "You forgot the baby Jesus set for under the tree."

Gabby kept the little manger set in her bedroom. I didn't know if I should go in there to get it. It had always been Gabby's private place, and nobody ever went in without an invitation. I'd only been in her room a few times in my entire life.

The first time had been when I was about five, and I was sure I'd found Ali Baba's cave. Old picture magazines were piled up in every corner and on top of her dresser. Clothes that needed mending were stacked on top of the magazines. Purses lay on top of the clothes. There must have been five or six old clocks, some actually ticking. Old dolls that Gabby was going to fix up someday were propped here and there, looking at you with drooping eyelids and faint smiles. A toaster peeked out from under the bed, and the walls were nearly covered with old paintings and spotted mirrors.

The bed was stacked with quilts and blankets and clothes that Gabby was thinking about wearing or maybe clothes that she had just worn. Gabby was little and thin, smaller even than me, and she always wore her clothes in layers, sometimes as many as four sweaters at a time. When I was a little kid, I was fascinated by this and once I wore seven shirts to school. I had arranged them so that I started with a turtleneck and then had collar inside collar inside collar.

But I needed the manger set, so I slipped into Gabby's room.

I stood inside with my back against the door and looked around. I had never been in there by myself before. But everything was the same as it had been when Gabby was alive. The covers were thrown back on the bed as if she'd just gotten up. Balanced on the crowded bedside table was her flowered teapot and a matching teacup stained with the last tea she drank. It felt as though Gabby had just left or might be walking back in any minute. I began to feel very strange. Then I realized that I was feeling strange because I had forgotten to breathe since I'd come in.

After breathing—a lot—I picked my way across the room to the closet. That seemed the most logical place for the crib set to be. But once I stood looking at the boxes and bags and tottering piles of things in Gabby's closet, I didn't know what to do. It didn't seem right for me just to rummage through them.

Then it came to me: Why not? If Gabby had been there, she'd have said, "Hop to it, Nick. Christa and Rudy are waiting." I knew Gabby. Just because she was dead didn't mean she had suddenly become someone I didn't know.

"Thanks, Gabby," I whispered. "Now if you could just show me where you put the manger set."

Believe this or don't, but just as I said that, a stack of picture frames, photograph albums, old newspapers, and sweaters slowly toppled over. At the bottom was a cardboard box with Gabby's printing on it: CHRISTMAS NATIVITY SCENE.

I grabbed the box and was shoving the rest of the pile back in the closet when something caught my eye. An apron.

It was a brand-new apron, with the price tag still on it. Gabby always picked up her aprons for a quarter at rummage sales. She liked the cheerful plaid kind with a big bib front. This apron just had the skirt part. It was white with lace trim, and all over the front were different plants and flowers with their Latin names.

There are some things you just know. And I knew that Gabby had bought this apron for Ma's Christmas present. Which was strange, because Gabby was the only one in the house who wore aprons. I folded it up very small and took it to my bedroom, where I put it in the bottom drawer. I would think about it later.

I was setting up the crib scene under the tree when Rudy crawled over, leaned up against me, and started sucking one of his shoelaces. Then Christa came in and sat down on my other side. "Primrose is riding the cake platter again," she said glumly.

I arranged a little wooden shepherd next to two of his sheep.

"Now what?" I said. "What's she worried about?"

A long time ago, Gabby found this silly birthday cake platter at a rummage sale. It's got a round plate that sits on top of a music box. You set a birthday cake on the platter, wind it up, and the plate part turns around and around while the music box part tinkles out "Happy Birthday to You." Whenever Primrose is upset, I mean *really* upset, she goes and sits on the platter. It's defective or something, so her weight always makes the thing go. The silly rabbit sits on the silly cake platter going around and around and around until she feels better.

"She's worried about Christmas," said Christa. "She says it's all very well and good—those were her exact words: 'all very well and good'—for you to decorate the house. But what about presents? I told her that Santa Claus would bring some, but she's not very much into Santa Claus, being a rabbit and all, and she wants to know about presents, from, like Ma. Ma always buys the best presents, but you know what she's like now."

Since I'd been worrying about the same thing, I didn't know what to say. When in doubt, change the subject. So I asked Christa what she wanted for Christmas.

"Loud clothes," she said.

I thought I heard wrong. "Did you say 'loud clothes'?"

"You think I'm joking when I say nobody ever sees me. But it's true. I'm the kind of person the teacher puts in the back row and forgets. Sometimes *weeks* go by and nobody talks to me at school."

"What about your friends?" I asked. "Meadow and Lucia."

"They just want an audience," said Christa. "I'm their friend because I let them talk and I tell them they're great. Dad's gone and Ma's not the noticing kind. There was only Gabby. Now nobody sees me."

She picked up one of the wise men and dusted him off.

She said, "You know, for a long time I didn't want anybody to see me, so it's kind of my fault, too."

"What do you mean, you didn't want anybody to see you?"

"Do you remember all the times we moved, Nick? We've been here for my second grade and part of third, but before that we moved around so much I never knew my address and phone number. I remember in first grade they thought I was really stupid because I couldn't tell them where I lived."

"Yeah, I remember," I said. "Dad was always looking for another job. Things were always going to be better at the next place."

"Well, they were never better for me," said Christa. "At first I would try to meet the new neighbor kids or find my way around the block, but I was always the new kid, always the one they teased. After a while, I just hoped they wouldn't see me."

The only comforting thing I could think of was, "Primrose sees you." Right on cue, Primrose came in, staggering a little like she does after riding the cake platter.

"Yes, Primrose does," Christa said, scooping her up and stroking the thick, shiny black fur. "But I want red jeans, or a huge black-and-white-and-orange sweater, or polka-dotted purple-and-yellow pajamas—something that's wild and noisy and loud. I'm ready for people to see me. The hand-me-downs I get from Aunt Meggie and the cousins are faded and blah. When Ma buys me clothes, they're black or brown or navy blue because they don't show dirt. But I want fuchsia or magenta or turquoise or salmon or chartreuse or . . . or . . . aquamarine!"

I didn't know what to say. Loud clothes?

"What do you want for Christmas, Nick?"

We live on a really tight budget, and what I wanted was so extravagant and outrageous and, well, impossible that I felt like a little kid asking for a real horsie. I started to say I didn't care what I got, but Christa had told me what she really wanted, and I figured I should be honest with her.

"I'd give anything for a pair of good binoculars," I said.

"Binoculars?" she said. "Oh! For spotting UFOs. But aren't they expensive?"

"Yeah, they are," I said. "So let's not even talk about it. Right, Rudy? Do you know what *you* want for Christmas, little guy?"

Rudy looked up, face wrinkling in concentration. I could tell he was getting ready to give us one of his words.

"Maybe," he said.

I waited. The thing about Rudy is that even though I *know* he's only got two words, he uses them so well that I'm always fooled into thinking he's going to really talk. When he didn't, I said, "Well, are you going to tell us what you want?"

"Later," said Rudy.

So there you have them, Rudy's two words: "maybe" and "later." He gets that from Ma. I'm sure that his next word will be "tomorrow."

I plugged in the Christmas tree lights, and the three of us sat there enjoying the winking lights and the red and green candles and the LEON on the mantel . . . LEON!

"Christa!" I yelled. "You fix those right now!" She got up and rearranged the letters.

. . . and the NOEL on the mantel and the manger scene under the tree. My favorite thing in the room, though, was still the music box. I got up and ran my fingers over it, feeling the carving and the silky varnish. What I really wanted to do more than anything was to lift the lid and hear "Joy to the World." I always used to shut my eyes tightly and wait for the silvery notes to turn into colored sparks behind my eyelids.

"Nick! You'd better dress Rudy again!"

I swept up Rudy and took him into his bedroom, where I looked for clothes that maybe he couldn't get out of. I needed strings I could knot and zippers I could turn around to the back so he couldn't reach them. I have to say, though, that we'd tried all this before. My brother is a baby Houdini.

When the three of us came back out into the living room, Peabody was sitting up and mumbling, "A great big kid. Which one of you is a great big kid? I saw him go through here a few minutes ago. I thought there were three of you. That must've been Leon, huh? Pretty big kid, that Leon."

It was the longest speech Peabody had ever made, and it was evidently very tiring, because several seconds later, there was a soft whuffling coming from the couch again. My old guinea pig used to sleep like that, too.

I figured I'd better go tell Dad he had to be more careful. But first I got Rudy settled for his nap and started Christa on a book. Then I stopped in the kitchen to pick up a couple of bananas and a package of crackers for Dad.

When I got downstairs, my father looked up and waggled his newspaper at me. "Nick, look at this! There are soldiers in South America that wear tuxedos when they go into battle." Sure enough, there was a picture of these guys on the battlefield in fancy suits and little bow ties . . . and carrying guns! I decided not to mention the tiny neon sign I could see in the background. I figure the picture was taken in Hollywood.

Just then I noticed that Dad's newspaper was acting funny. It was lying right next to him where he had set it down, but it was moving! Both Dad's hands were cradled behind his head. How was he making the paper move? Was this another kind of card trick?

Then Primrose stuck her nose out from under it. She hopped lightly onto Dad's lap and settled down to wash her face.

Dad looked a little sheepish. "It kind of likes me," he said.

I could understand that maybe Primrose gets bored when Christa is busy reading, but could she really like Dad? And how on earth had she managed to get down here? When I asked Dad, he looked shifty and said, "Well, you know how rabbits are. They can make themselves flat as paper and go right under the door."

I didn't want to tell him that was mice, not rabbits. It was bad enough telling him not to come upstairs in the daytime. He didn't want to hear it. "What am I supposed to do down here for days at a time?" he complained.

I wanted to say that he could always leave if he didn't like it, but I had a feeling that Dad wasn't into philosophical discussions of that nature.

Dad looked up with a crafty look on his face. "There wasn't much left in those bottles you had upstairs," he said. "I want some whiskey. If you can't manage that, I'll take beer. But I want something *now!*"

"How am I supposed to do that?" I asked him. "We haven't got anything more in the house, and I'm not old enough to buy it. Where can I get it?"

"That's your problem, isn't it? Just remember that *my* problem is that I need booze and I'm apt to get ornery if I don't get it."

I tried again to tell him how impossible it was. Actually, I knew how I could get him some beer, but I didn't want to do it.

Finally he said, his voice low and tight, "Just get it, Nick."

I shrugged. He was, after all, the eight-hundred-pound gorilla.

All the money I had in the world was about five dollars. I went upstairs to get it and then grabbed my coat, which I spent a few minutes trying to zip before I remembered that the zipper was broken. Ma had been meaning to fix it.

After finding my backpack, I went in to let Christa know I'd be back in an hour, and I ran out while she was still yelling, "I'm going to tell!"

At the grocery store, I prowled up and down the beer aisle, trying to look at least twenty-one and doing math in my head. I figured an average six-pack of beer cost about $3.50.

When I got back outside, I put three ones and two quarters in the envelope I'd brought along, and sealed it. Then I started walking the two miles to Tyrone's uncle's house. If I hadn't had other things on my mind, I would have enjoyed the walk. Fat snowflakes were drifting down, sticking to my coat and mittens for a few minutes before disappearing. I had to walk through downtown, and there was certainly no doubt about Christmas coming. Plastic wreaths with big bows hung from the streetlights, and all the windows were decorated with fake snow and candy canes and stuffed animals and fancy gift-wrapped "presents" that were really just empty boxes. Even though I knew that most of what I was looking at was fake and that the stores just wanted to get people inside so they would spend all their money shopping, I liked it. And anyway, the Salvation Army Santa Claus was real enough. He was ringing his bell energetically with one hand and wiping his red nose on his red mitten with the other hand. I know a reindeer who would have liked that nose.

As I got close to Tyrone's uncle's house, I started worrying about what I'd do if he or his wife had stayed home from work. I knew he stored extra beer in his garage to keep it cool. And I knew where he hid the garage key. I hated to do this because he was so good to Tyrone and me about his UFO magazines, but I didn't see that I had much choice.

I almost wish it hadn't been so easy. If only Tyrone's uncle had caught me in his garage. He would have had to call the police. And they might have questioned me under bright lights until I broke down and told them about my dad. And they would have come and taken him away. I felt kind of crummy, wishing that the police would come and haul my dad away. It was not one of the better moments in my life.

I loaded the beer into my backpack and left the envelope in its place. I had written on it:

Earthling: Accept our apologies. As we study your planet, we occasionally need samples of certain un-identified materials for our scientists to examine. You have been selected to be part of our study because of your interest in extraterrestrial life. Please accept our friendship and respect.

Knowing Tyrone's uncle, I was sure he would be *delighted* to have his beer stolen by aliens.

The six-pack banged into my back with every step I took. I was not cheerful by the time I unlocked the back door. I went directly to the basement, dumped the beer in front of my dad without a word, and went back upstairs.

And there I discovered that only *five* sugarplums were left on the tray. Five! A whole morning's work for five sugarplums.

"Christa!" I yelled.

She popped out from under the kitchen table and said, "What?" Like a shadow, Primrose hopped out beside her. Primrose was licking green frosting off her whiskers.

"You let that . . . that *rodent* eat the sugarplums?" I said.

"You leave Primrose alone," Christa said. "You've hurt her feelings. Just look at her." I shouldn't have looked, because it just made me madder. They say that human beings are the only mammals that can smile, but you couldn't prove it by me. That rabbit wasn't feeling hurt. She was feeling smug and superior and stuffed full of sugarplums, and she was *smiling*. My breath started coming faster, my hair began to lift on my head, and my skin tightened up all over.

I headed for the basement.

Dad tried to talk to me about some article where this cat learned to talk after it ate the family parrot, but I just ignored him.

I took out some new lumber, my tape measure, and the hand saw and started working. I had been making birdhouses to work off my frustrations since I was a little kid, so just about everyone I knew had gotten one. Every tree in our yard had at least one birdhouse, and we had more birds than Noah's ark. But this year I had a new twist: birdhouses with their own little stained-glass windows. I carefully unwrapped my pile of two-inch-square sun-catcher windows and began fitting the first one into a birdhouse.

Dad opened a beer and started playing solitaire. He didn't try to talk to me again, which was just as well. I was in such a bad mood that I felt I could match him, temper for temper. And that depressed me. I was scared of how mad I could get. What would happen if I ever let it all out? That's why I built birdhouses instead. So who is crazier? Someone who yells and screams and sometimes hits people? Or a guy who's built probably forty-seven birdhouses in his life and he's only thirteen years old?

CHAPTER SIX

 *December 22*

(*CONTINUED*)

While I was working at the tool bench, I got to thinking that maybe it would help Ma if dinner were ready when she got home. I know lots of kids at school who fix their own meals all the time. I had never had to because Gabby was always there. I capped up the glue tightly and went back upstairs, trying to remember how Gabby did things.

The first thing she did was easy. She put on her apron. It was still hanging on a hook behind the kitchen door, and after I put it on, I had the feeling that fixing dinner wasn't so impossible after all. I hadn't grown up on fairy tales for nothing. Cinderella had her ball gown, the Prince had his frog suit, Puss had those big boots, and I had Gabby's apron.

*    69    *

But here's the thing. You have this picture in your head of a dinner plate piled high with—let's say spaghetti and meatballs, a salad, and garlic bread. But what do you have to work with? A cardboard box that has been permanently sealed at the factory, frozen hamburger that you could pound nails with, and things in the vegetable drawer that look like a bad dream.

I was still down on the floor wrestling with the box of spaghetti when Ma got home. I could hear her talking to Peabody in the other room. I was pretty close to getting the end flap open. But when Ma walked into the kitchen, the screwdriver slipped and spaghetti sprayed out all over the room. It tap-tapped lightly across the floor and then rolled under the refrigerator, the table, and the cupboards.

Ma stood there for a few minutes, watching me pick up the spaghetti, before she shrugged out of her coat and threw it over the back of a chair. "I'll finish making dinner, Nick," she said. "What were you going to have?"

"Spaghetti and meatballs," I said, "with garlic bread and a salad."

She looked at me with—was it admiration?—and said, "That sounds great."

"Yeah, well, uh," I said, "the thing is, we don't have any spaghetti sauce."

"Oh, well, maybe I can—"

"And we don't have any bread. Or any lettuce. Or any garlic." I didn't even know what garlic looked like, so maybe we had some, maybe we didn't. But based on the general state of the kitchen, we probably didn't. "Actually, Ma, all we have is this kind-of-dirty spaghetti and that hamburger rock over there."

This is the place where it seemed to me Ma would get very tired and have to go to her room. But she didn't. She hesitated a minute, but then she opened the refrigerator door and said, "Let's see what we *do* have."

For the last couple of years, Gabby had done all the cooking at our house. But now that I saw Ma standing at the refrigerator door, I remembered other times, further back, when I had seen her doing these same things—taking cheese out of the refrigerator, turning on the stove, hunting for the right pan, refilling the saltshaker—talking to herself as she went.

I set the table, keeping an eye on her as I did it. That was a mistake. I nearly killed myself when I slipped on some spaghetti I'd overlooked. But I was curious to see what Ma would come up with for dinner. It was also nice being in the kitchen with her, just the two of us.

She cooked the hamburger until it got brown and crumbly. By then the spaghetti was done, so she mixed it and the hamburger in a big casserole dish, grated some cheese into it, added a can of mushrooms and salt and pepper. She put some spices in there, too, but I was too far away to read what they were. It didn't look great, actually, but Ma seemed to know what she was doing.

When I went to call Christa and Rudy for dinner, I realized that if Ma sat down to eat with us, it would be the first time we'd been together as a family since Gabby died. This was how things were going to be from now on. Without Gabby, it was just Ma and us kids. What would it be like? What if we didn't like it?

I was putting Rudy in his high chair when I suddenly thought, Chair! As soon as Ma turned around to take her casserole out of the oven, I sneaked Gabby's chair out of the kitchen into a corner of the living room. Very quietly, I moved the other chairs so they were spread out around the table.

Christa's favorite question is "What are you doing?" If she comes into the kitchen and I've got one piece of bread with peanut butter on it and I have the knife in the jelly jar, Christa will say, "What are you doing, Nick?" Really.

I only remembered this danger after I'd moved the chairs, but when I looked at Christa, she wasn't thinking about asking her stupid question. Her eyes were very big, and shining with tears. She knew what I was doing. Christa isn't *always* dumb.

And the casserole didn't look bad at all. Ma served us because the dish was too hot to handle. I saw her looking around for Gabby's chair, but she just went back to the stove to get the canned string beans she'd heated up. I was hoping she had forgotten Gabby's veggies-every-day rule.

I hunched over my plate and shoveled in the casserole.

The cheese was all melted and gooey, and long strings of it ran from my plate up to my chin. The casserole tasted even better than it looked. Nobody talked for a few minutes. I kept waiting for Ma to tell me to sit up straight and stop inhaling my food. That's what Gabby would have done.

Instead, Ma was choking. No, she was laughing. I followed her eyes to Rudy. The reason Rudy had been so quiet was that he was carefully hanging strands of spaghetti from between his lips. He had sort of a curtain of spaghetti running from one side of his mouth to the other. He looked like one of those walrus seals.

We all burst out laughing, including Rudy—unfortunately. His spaghetti sprayed out all over the table, except for one piece that hung from his lower lip. Pleased with all the attention, he made an O with his mouth and slowly vacuumed up the last strand, its little tail flicking him on the nose before it disappeared.

Still laughing, Ma leaned over and kissed him.

"Oh, yuck, you kissed him right on the lips, Ma!" said Christa. Ma quickly leaned the other way, toward Christa, and screwed up her face. "Yesssss, and now it is your turn, my little chickadee!"

Christa jumped up with a squeal and started running around the kitchen, "No! No! Don't kiss me on the lips!" But she wasn't running very fast or very far, and Ma caught her right away. After swinging Christa around, Ma gave her a big kiss—on the cheek.

Christa wiggled away and started running and squealing some more. You could see she really liked this game. But as she came around the corner, she knocked Rudy's milk off his tray with her elbow. It flew up over the table, hovered there for a minute, and then landed with a spin that sent milk splashing in a circle all around the table. It got every one of us. Amazing how much milk was in that little glass.

Rudy howled—not because he was wet, but because he likes to spill his own milk. Christa giggled, and Ma started mopping up.

Milk was running off the edge of the table and dripping into my lap, but all I could think was, What on earth would Gabby say if she could see this mess? She would never have let it happen in the first place, I knew. For a minute, I tried to figure out how Ma should have handled things. But Ma was Ma, and Gabby was Gabby. Things were going to be a little different from now on. Not better, not worse. Just different.

We were drying the dishes when the phone rang. What if it was for Dad? I jumped over Rudy, slid on some cooked spaghetti, and tore into the living room. Before the first ring had stopped, I was saying, "Hello?"

A gravelly voice said, "Yeah, gimme Monty."

Out of the corner of my eye, I could see Ma had followed me to see if the call was for her.

"Uh, he can't come to the phone right now," I said.

And then I realized what I'd said. If this had been a movie, this would be the place where the hero smacks his forehead and says, "Silly me!"

Ma was going to want to know who couldn't come to the phone. The only other "he" in the house, as far as she knew, was Rudy, and he didn't get many calls.

While I was standing there, brain ticking away uselessly, the guy on the other end said he'd call back and hung up.

The ticking brain caught. I said into the dead phone, "Well, I'm sure he'd want to talk to you, too. But the thing is, one of his reindeer bit him right on the lip. Yeah, Merry Christmas to you, too!"

I hung up, turned around very casually, and said to Ma, "Some little kid wanted to talk to Santa Claus. Heh, heh."

She looked a little doubtful, however, and when the phone rang a few minutes later, she said quickly, "I'll get it, Nick."

But it was only her friend Lurlene, asking Ma if she could bum a ride to work with her that evening. Christmas was really a busy time for florists, although Ma said it was nothing compared to Mother's Day and Valentine's Day. I remember how excited Gabby had been when Ma came home and said she'd gotten a job at a florist's. Ma not only sells flowers to people, she arranges bouquets and sets up the fancy displays in the big windows, too. As soon as Gabby heard about the job, she wanted to go see the place, but Ma kept saying there wasn't anything to see and, anyway, it would be too embarrassing to have her family standing around.

But one day, after Ma had been working there for a few

weeks, Gabby suddenly dropped the vacuum right in the middle of the living room floor and said, "Flowers! That's what this room needs. We'll go get some flowers for this room." She whipped off the towel she always wore around her head to protect her hair when she cleaned (her hair was pure white, and she was very proud of it) and yelled for us to get on our coats. She dressed Rudy and then bundled us all into the car, which was no easy job. We never got into the car with Gabby willingly.

After she fastened her seat belt, she used to grab the wheel so hard her hands got all stringy and her knuckles stood out. Then she'd make the car roar and snarl for a long time—"testing it," she said. Finally, without lifting her foot from the gas, she'd throw it into gear. The car would jackrabbit into the street, slamming us all back against the seats. One of Tyrone's dads is an electronics freak. He has VCRs, tape recorders, and stereos stashed all over the house. Most of them have a button called FAST FORWARD. That was how Gabby drove.

You could hear her muttering and hissing as the car weaved and dodged. There were sudden slammings on of the brakes and equally sudden darts into traffic immediately followed by great honkings of horns from other cars. She never took her hands off the wheel, which meant that she didn't use her turn signals. That got us even more honks as well as some rude gestures. What we minded the most was that she couldn't work the radio or the heater while she drove. The radio we could live without, but if the heat happened to be set on high, there it stayed for the whole ride, and never mind if our brains boiled over.

I remember once when Gabby took us to a church breakfast and this friend of hers said she never saw such quiet, well-behaved children. That's because we were still dazed from the car ride. Sometimes it took hours to recover.

Anyway, our visit to the florist shop was probably every bit as embarrassing as Mom had thought it would be. Gabby mostly stood around and said in a very loud voice things like "What a *lovely* window arrangement!" and "Who on earth has arranged this *fabulous* bouquet?"

Gabby would follow Ma around and, pointing to a tall arrangement of gladioli, for example, she would whisper, "Did you do that?" Ma soon learned that it was better to answer. If she didn't, Gabby just whispered more loudly. If Ma said yes, Gabby would walk around and around it and say she had never seen anything lovelier.

Finally Ma sidled up next to me and, while pretending to straighten out some vases, she hissed, "Tell Gabby you feel sick or something and have to go home. *Now.*"

I'm sure the owner was very surprised when we bought only a small bunch of daffodils, because Gabby had admired just about everything in the shop. Ma is usually kind of wishy-washy, but she laid down the law after that. We never visited her at work again.

Christa was pulling on Ma's sleeve now. "But, Ma," she

said, "you can't go back to work tonight. We were going to go look at the neighborhood Christmas lights."

But Ma really had to go, and she said she had arranged for Peabody to come back for a few hours after dinner. Peabody could take us instead.

Later, after Ma had left for work and it started getting dark, I went in and woke Peabody. "Ma said we could walk around the neighborhood and look at the Christmas lights," I said. Half-asleep, Peabody reached for Rudy's snowsuit. Personally, I thought that Peabody would be smarter to dress Rudy at the very last minute, but I didn't like to interfere. Peabody was looking at the mantel again and muttering, "Leon. Leon. That woman didn't mention a Leon." Peabody muttered for quite a while because Rudy's boots and snow-suit had to be put on four times.

Outside, the air snapped with cold. We walked over several blocks to where there were more houses with Christmas lights. The snow squeaked underfoot. Gabby always said you could tell when it was below zero because the snow squeaked.

We saw fat, cheerful red and green and blue lights, delicate white fairy lights, lit-up stars, wreaths, candles, and Santa Clauses. Lights were strung in bushes and trees, spiraled around pillars, draped across porches. One house had all the windows, the door, the whole roof outlined in lights. It looked like the kind of house a kindergarten kid would draw.

We came up behind a group of carolers and sort of joined

them. Unfortunately, these carolers took themselves very seriously. They sang in three- and four-part harmony and, as near as I could tell, they were all breathing from their diaphragms, which my music teacher, Mr. Hendon, was always trying to get us to do.

But I don't care how well they could sing. They were *not* nice people. If looks could kill, Christa would have dropped dead right there in the snow. So what if her voice is a little untrained, a little uncontrolled, a little—I might as well say it—a little shrill? At least her heart was in it. She sang so enthusiastically, her hat kept falling down over her eyes. I could see the carolers watching it and I knew what they were thinking: They were hoping it would fall way down over her mouth. For once, Christa couldn't say nobody noticed her.

We walked and gawked and sang until Rudy got tired. Peabody slung him over a shoulder, and we followed our frosty breath home.

After Rudy and Christa were in bed and Peabody had gone home, I went down to tell Dad it was a good time to make some of his phone calls. He must have been happy at the chance to get out of the basement because he took the stairs about four at a clip.

I was in the middle of a science fiction program on TV, so I didn't pay much attention to him, but he was in the kitchen for a long time. It occurred to me that I hadn't taken him any dinner.

I heard him dial the phone a few times and talk in a low

voice. Afterward he didn't seem to be in a hurry to go back downstairs. He wandered around the living room, picking things up and setting them down. There was a little wooden carving of a sheep on the mantel next to the music box.

"My old man did that," he said. "Whenever he was out of work, he'd sit around and whittle. Whittle and drink, mostly."

That grandpa died before I was born, so I never knew him. "What was he like?" I asked.

My dad shook his head. "I'll tell you what he was like. He was *strict*. I mean, that guy should have been a dog trainer. I spent more time in the corner than most spider-webs. I'll say this for him. He never hit me. But those corners were—"

The scrape of Ma's key in the door interrupted him. He disappeared so fast I didn't even hear the basement door. For a minute I wondered if he made himself flat as paper and went right under it.

Ma looked at the Christmas tree, and this time she didn't turn away. I said good-night and left her standing there.

Lying in bed that night, I decided that, bit by bit, Christmas *was* coming to our house. I only had two worries now. One was the presents. If Ma didn't come through, it wouldn't be a real Christmas. I wouldn't like to say this out loud, but I was *not* too old for presents. I wanted presents as much as Christa and Rudy did. It wasn't so much the presents themselves—although I have to admit that I am not wholly uninterested in presents—as Ma *giving* them, if that makes sense.

Because that was my second worry. Something was missing besides the presents, although it seemed to be all tied up with them.

Once when I was thinking about all this, I said to myself, "So. Big deal, Nick. You don't get any presents. You're a big boy now. You can live without presents." That's when it dawned on me that presents mean a lot more than just *things*. Behind the presents is something else.

Imagine that this family gets up on Christmas morning. Maybe they go to church. They come home and they look at their tree. They read the newspaper. Maybe they have a big dinner. But what? Let's say they all really love each other. What do they do about it? Do they talk? Well, that's nice, but I suppose they talk the rest of the year, too. Do they hug each other? Kiss each other? That's weird, just for no reason in the middle of the day, but I suppose that's okay. What I'm getting at here is, How do they show that they love each other?

Now with presents, they could save up their money, spend a lot of time finding the perfect present or making something. Then they could wrap it up, thinking about the person the whole time, tie a floppy red bow on it, and write the person's name in big letters on a little tag. With presents you can show people how you feel.

I really needed Ma to think about me—to think, "What

would Nick like for Christmas?" I wanted to see that she knew me well enough to pick out something I'd like. I wanted her to wrap my present, thinking the whole time about how tickled I was going to be when I opened it. I didn't care so much what she gave me, but I wanted her to think about me.

I know Christmas means different things to different people. I get embarrassed talking about it, but I know whose birthday it is, if you get what I mean. There are some kids at school who don't mind talking about religious stuff. One girl is always quoting from the Torah, and there's a guy who brings Jesus into the conversation every chance he gets. I admire them because their religion is so important to them that they don't care what anybody thinks of them. I'm sort of private about all that, but I'm just saying that if you had only one word to sum up Christmas, it would be "love." And I think presents are one way of showing that you love people.

Ma had been so strange since Gabby died, and I didn't know if she'd ever get back to normal. Doing a little Christmas shopping would be a good way of showing that she remembered us.

I was thinking so hard about Ma, I thought it was still my imagination when I saw her standing by my bed. Then I noticed she looked a lot like Mount St. Helens right before the big eruption.

"Nick," she said grimly, "I bought ten dollars' worth of groceries earlier tonight. They're all gone."

So that's what Dad had been doing in the kitchen.

I couldn't decide whether to act innocent ("Is that so?") or bewildered ("That's strange!") or mature ("Well, Ma, after all, I am a growing boy") or perhaps even humorous ("Hey, do you suppose Primrose has figured out how to get into the cupboards?").

Instead, I chose to be sympathetic. "Well, I'm sorry to hear that," I said. "Maybe the grocery store is still open at this time of—"

"Nick!" she roared. Well, I say "roared" because that's what it would have sounded like if it had been anybody else. With Ma, it was hardly enough to blow out the candles on a birthday cake. But what it meant was major trouble for me.

"Well, here's the thing," I began. "I mean, it's one of those . . . Well, you see that, don't you? It's all a question of how . . . And then, on the other hand . . ."

Sometimes this kind of flapdoodle works. But mostly it's only good for things like unmade beds and teasing Christa. Food that's missing is in a class all its own, I guess.

What can I say? She grounded me for two days. I wonder what she thought I did with all that food, anyway.

One more round to good old Dad.

CHAPTER SEVEN

# ❋ *December 23*

I was eating my second bowl of cereal the next morning when Tyrone started hammering on the front door. "Have I got something to tell you!" he burst out, as he shouldered his way in. "Good thing my mom kicked me out of the house or I'd still be doing chores."

"Which mom is that?" I asked. Once Tyrone drew me a chart of his original parents and all the people they had later married. I know that happens to a lot of kids, but what made it interesting in Tyrone's case was that every one of his parents and stepparents still lived right here in town, and he got shuffled around among all of them. I remember a football game where Tyrone's parents took up an entire row of the bleachers.

"Aw, it was Sheila," he said. "How was I supposed to know those cookies were for Christmas?"

"What cookies?" I said.

Tyrone bent over and unrolled his pant cuffs. He pulled out half a dozen Christmas tree cookies. "She didn't find these," he said.

He started to sit down, then jumped up and looked around. "Say, that rabbit isn't around, is it?"

I told him Christa and Primrose were still sleeping.

"Oh, good," he said. "But listen! You are never going to believe this! I mean, not ever! Hoo-boy!" He stuffed a cookie in his mouth, and said, "Fphum gree ophbekrezer . . ."

I knew what was coming, so it didn't matter that I couldn't understand the first half of his story. What I minded was being sprayed by Christmas-tree cookie crumbs.

". . . and on the envelope it said, 'Earthling: Accept our apologies.'" Tyrone had obviously memorized the message. As he rattled it off, I recited it right along with him. Halfway through, he realized he had an echo and he stopped. I continued alone: "Please accept our friendship and . . ." I trailed off.

You talk about life's great disappointments. Tyrone was a broken man. First I swore him to secrecy about my dad, then I explained the whole story to him.

I threw Tyrone a tangerine and started peeling mine. "What are we going to do about your uncle?" I said. "It's going to be pretty embarrassing if he tells people about this."

Tyrone spit a seed clear across the kitchen, where it landed in the sink. "No problem," he said. "My aunt is cool. She told him that if he talked about this, the aliens would never come back because of all the publicity. So he's keeping it quiet."

"But *she* doesn't believe aliens left that message, does she?" I asked.

"Naaah," said Tyrone, "but if you loved somebody, would you want to break their heart? This guy hasn't been so happy in years. Besides, if my aunt calls the police to report the stolen beer, my uncle will show the police the note and end up looking like a space ranger. Can you imagine a police officer buying the aliens bit?"

Christa wandered out, still half-asleep, and poured herself some cereal and milk. Tyrone and I talked about UFO movies and how phony they are, but after a while I noticed that Christa was looking pretty gloomy this morning.

"Hey, Christa," I said, "I've got a Christmas joke for you. Why does Santa Claus have three gardens?"

She thought a minute, then said, "I give up. Why?"

"Wait a minute!" said Tyrone. "Let me tell it. I know this joke." He frowned and started counting on his fingers.

Christa rolled her eyes, and said, "Why does Santa Claus have three gardens, Tyrone?"

Triumphantly Tyrone said, "So he can work, work, work!"

"What?" said Christa.

"Uh, wait a minute. No, no. It's so he can dig, dig, dig!" I didn't say anything. I knew Tyrone would eventually get there. This was not the first joke of mine he'd ruined.

"No, no! It's so he can hoe, hoe, hoe! Yeah, that's the ticket: hoe! hoe! hoe! Get it?"

"Ho, ho, ho," said Christa flatly.

"Yeah, that's what I said: hoe! hoe! hoe!" said Tyrone. "Isn't that great?"

"It sure is, Tyrone," said Christa, "that's why I'm saying 'ho, ho, ho'—because it's so funny, and I'm laughing. Get it?"

"Christa!" I yelled. "You quit it!" I can't stand it when she's mean to Tyrone. The two of them have never gotten along. I think it has something to do with Primrose.

Tyrone evidently felt he wasn't wanted. He levered himself to his feet.

"What the—"

The upper half of his body made a nearly impossible turn so he could look at the lower back half of his body—to examine the seat of his pants, to be precise.

I handed him a towel and mopped up the chair with a sponge. "Rudy isn't real good with a glass of milk yet," I said.

Muttering and grumbling, Tyrone trucked through the living room, giving Peabody a dirty look on his way. "Did you ever figure out what that is?" he asked. For a minute, we both stood there and studied the sleeping Peabody, looking for clues.

There were none.

When I came back from seeing Tyrone off, Christa was waiting for me. "I know you're mad at me, Nick," she said, "but I need you to help me. If you do, I promise I'll be super nice to Tyrone the next time he's here."

"I sure am mad," I said. "After all, Tyrone is my friend and . . ."

Christa held up one hand. "I *said* I'd be nice. I don't need the lecture."

"Okay, okay. What do you want?"

She pulled her other hand out from behind her back. She was holding a scissors, a comb, and a magazine with a picture of hair. Well, the hair was on a girl, but the main point of the picture was the hair. Christa wanted her hair to look like that hair—cut short to the chin and kind of curling under. It was not bad-looking hair.

Christa's, on the other hand—well, Christa had been trying to grow her hair for years, and I don't think she was meant to have long hair. Hers just got snarly and hung in little rats' tails down her back.

"Just in *case* I get loud clothes for Christmas," she said, daring me to say anything, "I want my hair to look nice."

I didn't have any problem with that, but I couldn't just cut her hair, no. We had to pretend we were a beauty parlor. Christa pulled a chair into the middle of the kitchen, wrapped her neck in a big dish towel, and set up a little tray with the scissors, comb, a hand mirror, and a glass of water (I was supposed to keep dipping the comb in there).

The worst of it was that she kept calling me Arturo. She said all the best beauty parlors had people with names like that. I said if we were going to be realistic, she could pay me. She stopped calling me Arturo after that.

It took nearly all morning because Christa said that if I didn't get it right, she was going to sneak into my room in the middle of the night and fix *my* hair.

While I was working away, I could hear Rudy laughing and giggling in the other room. Peabody must have been playing with him. I would have liked to have seen that.

Christa seemed happy with her hair—but then, she couldn't see the back of it very well. After I swept up the floor, I went downstairs to see if the glue on the birdhouses was dry where I had put in the stained-glass windows. Dad was working a word puzzle in one of his newspapers. Primrose gave me a disdainful look from Dad's lap.

"Boy, this is going to be the easiest hundred bucks I ever made!" Dad said, waving his pencil. "This word puzzle is so simple. I want you to mail it as soon as I get it finished."

I knew about those word puzzles from some kids at school who had done them. They were easy on purpose. After you and six million other people sent in the correct answer, they wrote everybody and said something like, "Wow! You have won! Unfortunately, there is a two-way tie between you and six million other people. Enclosed is a tie-breaking puzzle. After you have completed it, please return it (along with a five-dollar processing fee) to see if you are the Grand Prize

Winner." After that round, you were tied with only about two million people, and it would cost ten dollars to process *that* tiebreaker. If Dad gave me his puzzle to mail, I'd see that it got put in a mailbox, but I didn't think I'd waste a stamp on it.

The glue on my birdhouses was dry all right. In big gloppy streaks down the side. I could have cried. Dad set aside his paper and came over to see what I was groaning about.

"The glue ran," I said. "Look. I must have used too much. Now the stain won't take. And these streaks look terrible."

Dad said, "Here, give me a little sandpaper, and I'll take care of it." He seemed glad to have something to do. As I left, he was already busy: *skritch, skritch, skritch.*

I went upstairs and called Christa and Rudy for lunch. As I spread the peanut butter on the bread, I thought to myself that if Christa had even one little complaint about lunch, I was going to make a peanut butter sandwich with her head in the middle.

But instead she said, "What's that noise?"

*Skritch, skritch, skritch.*

"I don't hear anything," I said.

*Skritch, skritch, skritch.*

"You *have* to hear it, Nick. It's coming from the basement, see?" She opened the basement door and started down the stairs.

"Oh, *that* noise!" I said, grabbing her arm and then trying to turn it into a friendly hug. "Those are termites, and I think they're real vicious if you disturb them when they're working."

"Termites!" she shrieked. "Ugh! They'll chew down the whole house. We learned at school that one termite queen can produce over five hundred million baby termites. We've got to stop them!"

Good grief, is there no peace in this world?

Then I noticed Primrose had come up from the basement and was all huddled up on the floor with her front paws over her head. That is the most sarcastic rabbit I have ever seen.

By the time I calmed Christa down—I told her there were good termites and bad termites, and we had the good kind—I felt pretty wrung out. I wasn't sure I would live until Christmas.

When I took Dad a new jar of peanut butter and some bread, he looked at it glumly and said, "At least in prison there was a little variety to the food."

He looked up hopefully and asked, "What's for dinner tonight?"

Well, that was a tough one. If I told him the truth—which was "nothing"—he might get mad. If I made up something and then couldn't deliver, he might also get mad.

While I was still turning over the possibilities in my mind, he said, "Why don't I fix dinner? I like messing around in the kitchen. Your ma used to say I could make a gourmet meal out of nothing."

"Well, you've come to the right place," I said, "because that's about what we have up there. Ma's missing ten dollars' worth of groceries, remember? But how can you fix dinner without anybody seeing you?"

"It's just you kids and that baby-sitter, right?" he said. "Since the baby-sitter sleeps all the time, all you have to do is keep the kids out of the kitchen for about half an hour later this afternoon."

"Yeah, okay. The only thing is," I said, "I think it's going to be easier for you to fix dinner than it is for me to keep Christa and Rudy out of the way."

"Just do a few magic tricks for them," Dad said. He poked me with his elbow. "Remember when you and I used to do magic tricks together?"

"Yeah," I said, "but you did all the tricks and I just passed the hat. You taught me a couple of tricks, but I'm not very good. I might be able to keep Christa and Rudy occupied for, oh, say, two or three minutes."

"Hmm," said Dad. "Well, maybe you could read them some of my newspapers. Here's a story they'd like. See, this fellow could fly through walls. He was what you'd call a guru—sort of a modern-day wizard. But once when he was giving a demonstration, he flew through the first two walls and then—get this!—he lost his concentration and he got *stuck* in the third wall. It says here that most of his face and his right hand got through the wall, but the rest of his body is still trapped in there. Here's what a famous scientist said about it: 'This is a tragedy of the highest magnitude.' Isn't that something? Isn't that just something?"

You could see Dad really liked that story. Maybe Christa and Rudy would, too. Afterward, I could read to them about Aladdin and his lamp and . . .

"Hey, Dad!" I said. "I know. *You* could be a wizard." I explained my plan to him. He wasn't crazy about it, but he didn't have a better idea. "I'll be ready for you right around four-thirty," I told him. "When you're finished, rap on the wall three times so I know the coast is clear, okay?"

I was halfway up the stairs when he called out, "Say, I don't suppose you have a dishwasher up there?"

"A dishwasher? Well, since Gabby died, I guess I'm the chief dishwasher, but why do you—"

"No, no," he said, "I mean a machine. One of those things that washes the dishes for you. Because, see, I've just been reading about how you can cook in the dishwasher. You just wrap the food up and run the dishwasher through its cycles. This chef has some of his best dishwasher recipes in the newspaper here—like, look at this one for Dishwasher Veggies."

Dishwasher Veggies? Gag. Was he kidding?

"I'm sorry, Dad," I said, "but you'll just have to make do with the stove." I left him mumbling about people with no imagination.

It was a slow afternoon. I have this theory that the faster you *want* time to go—like, say, before your birthday or before Christmas—the slower it actually goes. It has something to do with negative energy or centrifugal force or maybe just plain cosmic orneriness.

While Rudy took his nap and Christa and her friend Meadow played at Peabody's feet, I talked to Tyrone on the phone for a couple of hours. We didn't talk the whole time. Sometimes I set the receiver down and got myself a snack or Tyrone did chores for his mom while I took the handset on the phone apart. It was a pretty boring conversation, actually. But eventually Rudy got up, Meadow went home, and it was time for Dad to start dinner.

Christa and Rudy could hardly believe their good luck when I offered to read them a story. They really went over the top when I dragged the pillows off all the beds to make a comfortable nest in the living room for us. When they were settled, I started reading *Aladdin and the Wonderful Lamp*. You could just see them getting into the magic of the plot.

Afterward, I gave them both a long, considering look. "I think you two are old enough to know a big secret," I said. "But you must promise never to tell anyone else what I am about to tell you."

This is the point where normally Christa would say, "Yeah, I know you, Nick. Big secret, ha!" But after hearing *Aladdin*, she was still half in fantasyland, which is what I was counting on. Even Primrose looked interested.

"I have—are you ready for this?—a wizard of my very

own." I stopped to let them appreciate this amazing information.

"A long time ago," I continued, "I found a piece of magic. With it, I can call up a wizard who will obey my every command."

"Let's see! Let's see!" cried Christa. Slowly and dramatically, I held out my hand. On it lay a roundish, dull orange lump. Before they could look at it too carefully, I closed it in my fist. I didn't *think* they would realize it was only a hundred-year-old piece of cheese from the back of the refrigerator, but I didn't want to take any chances.

"Oh, Wizard!" I called.

From the direction of the kitchen came a deep voice: "Yesmasteryourwishismycommand." You could tell Dad's heart wasn't really in this.

Christa's eyes got so big, I could see the whole Christmas tree in them. "Let's ask for a million dollars," she whispered. "Or for a new house. Or . . ."

Oops.

"Wait a minute," I said, "This is my wizard, and I don't want to wear him out. Let's save the big stuff for later. Right now, I just want you to see how it works. I'll have him do something like—oh, I know! We'll have him fix dinner!"

"Fix dinner!" said Christa. "Fix dinner? A wizard? You're going to use a wizard to fix dinner when we could be getting a million dollars?"

Fortunately, Dad came to my rescue. Showing a little more

interest this time, he said, "It shall be so, Master. I will prepare dinner. But remember, if anyone looks upon my face, I will disappear, never to be seen again." And he began banging pans and opening drawers.

Christa slumped down. Rudy's head swung from me to Christa and back again. "You blew it, big brother," Christa said. "Right this very minute, we could be sitting on a pile of one-hundred-dollar bills." She patted the floor on either side of her in disbelief.

While Christa was mourning her lost millions, I laid out the paper and scissors and glue we needed to make the red and green paper chains. I told Rudy we had to wrap the finished chains around his arms. This was one of my better ideas because, in that position, Rudy couldn't undress himself or wander into the kitchen.

For an hour we cut and pasted. From the kitchen came noises and good smells and even a little humming. Christa frowned once and said, "Did you hear that? It sounded like someone flipping open a can of beer."

Another time, we heard something drop, and then there were some words that Gabby always called blasphemous and Ma called taking the Lord's name in vain.

"Your wizard *swears*?" asked Christa. "And drinks beer?"

"What do you want for nothing?" I said. "When you find a wizard just lying around, you don't complain because he's not top of the line."

"Where's your magic thing?" asked Christa suddenly. "I want to see it."

I looked around me. I had set it down when we started making the paper chains. Christa and I crawled around on the floor looking for it. But the deed was already done. Primrose was licking orange crumbs from her whiskers when we finally thought to check on her. For once, that rabbit did the decent thing by me.

Christa, of course, saw the whole thing in a different light.

Her eyes shone with wonder and awe. She reverently gathered Primrose to her and said, "Primrose is now a magic rabbit."

A magic rabbit? Give me a break.

We had just finished draping the paper chains around the windows and doors when there were three loud knocks on the kitchen wall. Christa and Rudy froze.

"Don't worry," I told them. "The wizard always does that just before he goes back to wherever he lives."

Christa grabbed my arm. "Don't let him go back! We haven't asked him for any big things yet!"

"Too late, Christa," I said. "When that guy gets ready to go, there's no stopping him."

CHAPTER EIGHT

✳ **December 23**

(*CONTINUED*)

The three of us went into the kitchen to see what Dad—I
mean, the wizard—had fixed for dinner. I think Christa and
Rudy were expecting something with shooting stars and
glitter and puffs of smoke. But I had no complaints. Dad
had left a meat loaf and a vegetable casserole in the oven.
On the shelf were a bowl of carrot sticks and a plate full of
cranberry muffins.

I talked Christa into helping me clean up the kitchen and
set the table. We used some leftover construction paper to
make red and green place mats. Then we made name tags
and decorated the napkins. I even took some of the tree ornaments and arranged them in a breadbasket in the middle of

the table. It looked so nice, I wanted to take a picture of it.

"Now remember," I said to Christa, "the wizard is *our* secret. Don't tell anyone about it, okay?"

Christa nodded. Then she gave me a funny look. "I suppose I shouldn't tell anybody about the termites, either."

"Uh, right," I said.

"Or about yesterday when you left the house without telling anybody," she added.

"Uh, yeah, that, too," I said.

"I think something funny's going on around here," she said, bending down to pick up Primrose. As I said, Christa tunes in pretty well to the big picture.

I fished Rudy out from under the table and got him dressed just as we heard Ma at the front door. The door slammed a second time, which meant that Peabody had gone home.

I whipped Gabby's apron off the hook and put it on. I wasn't going to tell any lies, but if Ma looked at the dinner and then saw me in the apron and got the wrong idea, I couldn't help that.

Ma stood in the kitchen doorway, pushing her hair behind her ears. She looked surprised at the fancy table and the food. But then she noticed Gabby's apron.

"Oh, yeah, I'm sorry, Ma," I said, untying the apron and pulling it off. "You should be the one to have Gabby's apron." I held it out to her, but her hands made little dusting motions in front of her, and she shook her head.

The meal was delicious, and it was nice eating as a family for the second night in a row. Then Christa had to ruin everything. "Ma," she said. "Can I have Gabby's bedroom now? I'm tired of sharing a room with Rudy, and this way we'll each have our own room."

Ma set her fork down very carefully. She wiped her mouth with her napkin. She stood up and looked at Christa as though she wasn't sure who Christa was. "Gabby's . . . bedroom?" she said.

She walked slowly out of the kitchen, and I could hear her going down to the end of the hall, and then the little *snick* of Gabby's bedroom door opening. Then I didn't hear anything for a long time.

I felt cold, inside and out. One winter we visited my cousins in Chicago. I was trying to sleep with a slippery comforter. Comforter, ha! It was the most uncomfortable night of my life. I'd pull it up over my shoulders and my feet would stick out. If I covered my feet, my shoulders were cold. Then the whole thing would start slipping off the side of the bed. I'd pull it up and it'd head south, or north, or any direction where I wasn't. I felt that way now. Every time I thought I had a hold on things, they'd slip away. And the harder I tried to make everything work, the colder I got.

After dinner, I went downstairs to stain the birdhouses. It must have been having Dad there that reminded me, but I thought about how I got started on birdhouses.

One day when I was about five or six, Dad came roaring into the kitchen, waving his watch and heading straight for me. I forget some of this, I think because I don't like remembering it. I know he called me a brat and a few other things. He said I had smashed the crystal on his watch. At first I was scared, but I knew I hadn't touched his watch. And so, after a while, I got mad.

He wouldn't believe me, no matter what I said. Even Ma tried to say that maybe it had happened when he was out drinking the night before and he just hadn't noticed until the next day.

That took the heat off me for only a minute while he snarled at Ma. And all the while I was getting angrier and angrier at being accused of something I hadn't done. I felt like one of those frogs that swell up. Would I finally just go *pop!* and burst? Or would I start screaming and yelling like Dad?

Then a warm, rough hand took mine. Gabby led me out of the kitchen, keeping herself between my dad and me. We went down to the basement and sat on the bottom step.

Gabby held her arms way wide and said, "Are you this angry, Nick?"

Oh, how good that felt! Yes, I was that angry. Maybe even more!

Gabby said, "There's nothing wrong with being angry, Nick. But it doesn't feel very good, does it? This is what we'll do."

She lifted me up onto the splintery old tool bench that hung along one wall. Then she rummaged in a pile of wood scraps until she found what she needed. Gabby cut out the wood for my first half dozen birdhouses. She also taught me how to glue them together.

After a while, it got so that I could do them by myself, and I've been getting better and better over the years. In fact, the birdhouse I made for Tyrone for Christmas this year is a real winner. It's almost an exact replica of a UFO that landed outside Denver a couple of years ago. The great thing is that the design makes a natural birdhouse because birds can perch all around the outside rim or they can go inside through half a dozen different doors. I think he's going to love it.

I knew it wasn't possible in the middle of winter, but I seemed to be hearing thunder. Dad and I looked at each other, and I went upstairs to see what was going on. The "thunder" was Ma pushing furniture around in the living room.

You have to understand that Ma had never done anything like that in her whole life. I must have looked surprised because she said hesitantly, "It's just that . . . well, with the Christmas tree in here, things aren't . . . I thought maybe if I arranged it like . . . but I'm not sure if . . ."

I told her it was wonderful, just what the living room needed, was I ever glad she thought of it, et cetera.

"Oh, do you really think so?" she said. "Hmm, I wonder

if this chair would fit in my bedroom. . . ." She staggered off, carrying the fat green chair.

The phone rang just then, but Ma and the chair were sort of wedged into her bedroom doorway, so I was able to get to it first.

"Lemme talk to Monty," said a hoarse voice. (Where does Dad get these people?)

I looked to see if Ma could hear, and I whispered into the phone, "He can't talk right now. Can he call you back?"

"Yeah, tell him to call Lenny."

I hung up just as Ma came back to see who it was.

"It was for me," I told her. I could see her immediately tune out as she checked to see how the living room looked without the green chair. "Yeah," I continued, "that was Snow White. She just wanted to say hello. These girls, they're calling me all the time."

"Mmm," said Ma, returning to her room.

It was a good chance to run down and tell Dad about Lenny's call. But Dad was all excited about an article in one of his papers, and he made me listen while he read the whole thing out loud. It seems that in some parts of the world these people take eggs and stuff them inside a fish. Then they stuff the fish inside a chicken, the chicken inside a sheep, and the sheep inside a whole camel. That's not the worst part. The worst part is that then they eat it. I got out of there as soon as I could.

On my way to bed I stopped to rearrange the NOEL on

the mantel. Then I patted the music box. Whenever I saw it, I felt hopeful, although there wasn't any reason to be, as far as I could tell.

As I pulled down my covers, I thought about how our family used to revolve around Gabby. Now that she was gone, it looked as if I got to be "it." There I was, taking Dad his food, booze, and telephone messages and keeping his secret, doing the baby-sitting that Peabody got paid for, listening to Ma and worrying about dinner when she should have been doing it. I did not apply for this job, and if I'd known there was an opening, I would have done something easier, like being a door-to-door salesman for earthworm cookies.

CHAPTER NINE

## ❊ *December 24*

The next morning was the day before Christmas, and we were all up early. Not too excited or anything. Ma had gone off to work muttering about people who waited until the last minute to buy their poinsettias, and Peabody—well, Peabody, installed in the usual manner on the couch, was a living, breathing home decorating accessory. Some people use plants or coffee table books or fancy candlesticks to give their living rooms that "attractive, lived-in look." We had Peabody.

After I fixed some cereal for the three of us, we hung our stockings from the hooks hidden under the fireplace mantel. I plugged in the Christmas tree lights and straightened up the living room. It looked so nice I didn't want to leave the room, so I pulled Rudy onto my lap and read him "The Night Before Christmas."

Toward the end, Christa came and sat next to me. When she leaned her head on my shoulder, I looked at her quickly. That wasn't like Christa. Neither were the big tears rolling down her face.

"Ma hasn't got any presents hidden in her room," she said. "I looked everywhere. There isn't going to be a Christmas, is there?"

"There is always a Christmas," I said. "Even if there are no presents, no tree, no cookies, no songs, Christmas always comes. If we want it to.

"Besides"—I poked her gently with my elbow—"we're the Christmas family."

She looked up, surprised out of her tears. "What do you mean?"

Then I was surprised. "Hasn't anybody ever told you about our names?" I asked. "I thought you knew."

She shook her head. I settled Rudy more comfortably on my lap and said, "It's like this. When Gabby was just a tiny baby, somebody brought her to the orphanage in a little basket and left her. It was Christmas Day. They never found out where she came from. But she was such an angel that the people at the orphanage decided to name her after the Christmas angel, Gabriel. Since she was a girl, they called her Gabriella. For a last name, they chose 'Christmas.' "

"Christmas! You can't have a name like Christmas!" said Christa.

"Yes, you can," I told her. "You just look in any big phone book and you'll find a couple of them. Jack Christmas. George Christmas. Martha Christmas. Anyway, because of Gabby everybody in our family has a Christmas name. Like Ma's name is . . ."

"Joy! Ma's name is Joy!" she said. "And, oh! I see. I'm Christa for Christmas and you're Jolly Old St. Nicholas and Rudy is . . ."

"Right!" I said. "Rudolph the Red-Nosed Reindeer. Most people never catch on about our names. It's the family secret. That's why Christmas is always special for our family."

Christa still looked a little doubtful, so I put one hand in hers and one in Rudy's and led them into the kitchen. I got out the box of toothpicks and said, "If we pick out an even number of toothpicks, everything will work out just fine for Christmas. If we pick out an odd number, it won't."

I reached in and fingered four toothpicks. I laid them in Christa's hand and told her to count them.

A smile spread slowly across her face. "Four! Oh, great! Thanks, Nick! Hey, Rudy, you want to play school?"

It felt good to pass on the torch to the new generation. I had basically outgrown the toothpicks, but I was afraid to stop altogether. Now Christa could take over the job.

I wandered back into the living room. As I looked at Gabby's music box, I realized that Christa and Rudy were busy playing school and Peabody was asleep. I'm not sure I was actually planning to play the music box. Ma had sounded pretty serious about not touching it. Who knows what bad fortune I might bring down on our heads by disobeying?

I'll tell you what kind. The immediate kind. Because when I picked it up, Peabody suddenly snorted and I dropped it!

There was a rug in front of the fireplace, so it didn't get scratched or dented, but there was an unpleasant little *ping* when it hit the ground. And when I tried to wind it, the key just flopped loosely around and around.

As I fiddled with it, I remembered the other time Gabby's music box broke. It was a late Christmas afternoon, and the windows were getting dark. The only light besides the Christmas tree lights came from two fat candles on the fireplace mantel. The music box was sprinkling its silvery notes all over the room as I worked on a new puzzle near the tree. Ma and Gabby were picking up wrapping paper and ribbons.

Suddenly Dad was there. Even then I didn't run to him. I don't think I ever did after I was about two years old and discovered that he didn't like it. But from my spot on the floor, I could smell the bad smell and see that his eyes were bleary.

I don't remember what he said. But I remember the crash and the way the music box stopped in the middle of a note when he threw it on the floor.

The next Christmas, Gabby brought the music box out

of her room, and it worked just as it always had. Nobody ever said a word about what had happened to it.

Now it was broken again. Like father, like son? I carefully eased out the insides. I closed the lid and left the box on the mantel. With any luck, nobody would look inside.

I decided to take the parts to Dad. He knew a lot about car engines. Maybe he could fix it.

But the minute Dad saw my legs coming down the stairs, he started talking and waving his paper excitedly. "Look at this, Nick! A genuine diamond—I mean guaranteed genuine!—for only one dollar. Has my luck ever turned now! What do you want to bet I can sell this thing for a small fortune? I don't suppose you have a dollar on you?"

With my free hand, I turned my right-hand pocket inside out. Nothing. Then he saw what I had in my other hand. He made a noise sort of like a laugh.

"Don't tell me," he said. "I'd recognize that little gizmo anywhere. I once spent two weeks of my life working on it. I could fix it in my sleep."

After explaining what had happened, I left Dad tinkering with the music box parts and went upstairs to wrap my presents. But first I had to find something to keep Christa and Rudy out of the way while I did—and I knew just what would do it.

Gabby had this tall, old-fashioned dresser made out of bird's-eye maple, and on rainy days she would pull out a couple of the dresser drawers for us to "organize." Although she was neat as a pin in the rest of the house, Gabby was a pack rat in the privacy of her bedroom. So when she asked us to sort her drawers, we loved it. The things we found in them! Peppermint candies, colorful shells, a broken brooch, lengths of handmade French lace, jet beads, old watches, wheat-back pennies, decks of cards that never had fifty-two, feathers, a smooth striped stone, rainbow spools of thread, a screwdriver with a cracked handle, and misshapen, mysterious things that even Gabby could no longer identify. Nobody noticed or cared that after an entire day of being "sorted," Gabby's drawers looked exactly the same as they had that morning.

So I settled Christa and Rudy with a drawer apiece, went in my room, shut the door, and began wrapping my birdhouses. I also wrapped the apron and marked it TO MA FROM GABBY.

When I carried my presents to the living room to put under the tree, Christa said, "Nick, I keep hearing music. Rudy hears it, too, don't you, Rudy?"

Rudy shrugged and said, "Maybe."

"Well, I do, and I'm not crazy," said Christa, and she burst into tears. Primrose came running over and jumped into her lap.

Poor Christa. Everything was really getting to her.

I sat down beside her and said, "They say that on Christmas Eve a few very special, very sensitive, and very good people actually hear the heavenly choirs of angels singing. You must be one of the lucky few."

She brightened up right away, and I could see she felt better. I, on the other hand, felt lousy. What kind of a person could go from being an amateur, once-in-a-great-while type of liar to a world-class professional in a matter of days?

I went downstairs to tell Dad to keep the music box quiet if he could. But he was finished with it.

"Just slip that back inside. It'll be fine," he said. But he didn't give it to me right away. He stood there, holding it and looking at me sideways. "Do you remember the last time this broke?" I nodded and looked away, embarrassed and uncomfortable.

"Yeah, well," he said, "I always had a hard time with holidays. Some people get a little crazy during the full moon. With me, it's holidays."

He stopped and thought. "Of course, I also had a hard time when it wasn't a holiday. Things really got to me, you know? When I was out of work or when we'd been in the same place too long or when you and Christa were little rug rats and I was always tripping over you—things would build up in me, and I'd just lose it."

He put his hands in his pockets, lowered his head to his chest, and said with a sigh, "I was not what you'd call a great human being."

"Oh, Dad!" My eyes prickled, and I wanted to touch him, but I wasn't sure if he'd like that. For one strange click of time, I was huge, much bigger than he was, glowing with love and sympathy, and I bent down and surrounded him with arms that shimmered with light. In a second, the picture was gone, but the feeling stayed with me. I would never like some of what my dad had said and done over the years, but I knew that things would always be different between us after seeing him this way.

"Hey, Dad, it wasn't *that* bad, you know. There were good times, too."

He brightened up. "Yeah? Like what?"

"Well, picnics, for one thing. You and Ma were the picnickingest people."

"That's right," he said. "We were good at picnics. Nothing ever bothered me when I was sitting on a blanket eating your ma's potato salad and watching you kids play on the grass."

"And Christmases weren't all bad, either," I said. "Remember the year you and I drove up north to chop down our own tree? I never forgot that. I tried to fit my little boots into the big tracks you left in the snow, hoping that someday I'd be as big as you. I think we kept that tree up until Valentine's Day, we were so proud of it."

"Yeah." Dad was definitely looking more cheerful now. He said, "Do you remember that crazy finch we bought your ma for Christmas one year?"

How could I forget? Dad and I had gone Christmas shopping together, although I got the feeling that he was not too pleased to have me along. Ma must have made him take me. He looked longingly at the bars we passed on the way downtown, and I knew that if I hadn't been with him, he would have stopped.

When we passed a pet shop window full of cats and dogs and birds, I more or less lost control of my feet and found myself pasted right up against the glass.

Dad noticed that the little zebra finches were on sale, and he thought that one of them would be a great Christmas present for Ma. We went inside to get a better look. They were the cutest little birds—so small they would have fit in my six-year-old hand. They had bright orange beaks and feet, black-and-white-striped tail feathers, rust-colored spots on their cheeks, fat white stomachs, and beady black eyes.

And they were quiet. "There's nothing worse than a yapping bird," Dad had said. "These little guys seem pretty decent."

We picked out what we were sure was the cutest, smartest bird, bought a cage and some bird feed, and then Dad figured out a way to stop at a bar after all.

"We've got to leave this bird somewhere until Christmas so your ma doesn't see it," he explained. "I know the bartender at this place on Wilson, and he'll keep the bird for me until Christmas Eve." So while Dad and his friend Pete were discussing the bird—and the weather and several football games—I sat on a high stool drinking a Coke and hoping the bird didn't die before Christmas from breathing the smoky air in that place.

According to Pete, the bird didn't say a word the whole time it was staying with him. Pete swore that was the truth. And, of course, when Dad and I had seen the bird in the pet shop, it hadn't made a peep.

But on Christmas morning, as soon as Ma unwrapped the cage, the bird opened its tiny beak and let out a piercing *Chirp, chirp, chirp, CHIRP! Chirp, chirp, chirp, CHIRP!*

And it never stopped.

Ma was delighted with it. Of course, that was only in the first few minutes. She hugged Dad and said, "I love it."

Dad cupped his ear and said, "What?"

Ma said loudly, "I *said*, I *love* the *bird!*"

After that, it seemed somebody was always saying, "What?" and we began yelling at one another to be heard over the bird. It never shut up. And our apartment was not very big. No matter where you went, you could hear the bird. By the end of Christmas Day, our eyes were glazing over and we were too listless to eat. And the bird never quit. *Chirp, chirp, chirp, CHIRP! Chirp, chirp, chirp, CHIRP!*

The next day, Dad and I went back to the pet shop—carrying a bird cage. There was a long line ahead of us, but we were willing to wait. I couldn't read that well yet, but Dad pointed out a sign over the cash register that said NO REFUNDS ON LIVE PETS.

"What other kinds of pets are there?" he said to me. "Dead pets?" I noticed that most of the people ahead of us were holding bird cages with cute little finches in them. None of them made a peep—the birds, I mean. Of course, the people weren't talking either. They looked about as dazed as we did. We didn't get our money back, but we talked the pet shop people into taking the finch off our hands. All in all, we figured it was a good day's work.

Still smiling about the finch, Dad looked down at the music box mechanism in his hand. And his smile faded.

"I'm glad you remember some good times, Nicky," he said. "Because they were just as real as the bad times. And just as important. Sometimes I forget that. But while I was working on this"—he nodded at the music box mechanism—"I got to thinking. This isn't the only thing I've ever broken. I've broken a lot of things. And I always seem to end up hurting people. I never mean to, you know. It just happens. All the time I was in prison, I dreamed about coming back here. Oh, I know. Your ma probably wouldn't let me. But I used to think how it would be if I were a little different, and she wanted me back."

I stood very still. It was strange to hear my dad talking like this.

"But you know what?" he said. "It's not time for me to come back yet. Maybe it never will be. I don't know."

He wound the music box mechanism and listened to it for a minute. I think he forgot I was there. He said slowly, "I've got some things to do first. I've got to get off the booze. I've got to do something about my temper, and I've got to figure out why I always end up in trouble."

He looked up then. "Being in this basement has been a weird experience, let me tell you. I've had a lot of time to think, and hearing all of you moving around upstairs—well, it's like I'm here, but I'm not here. All my life, people have been telling me that I've got to take responsibility for my own choices. I'd just think, Yeah, yeah, yeah. But for the first time, I kind of know what they mean. I know now that I have to change, and I really want to change. The problem is that I'm still at the thinking stage—I haven't actually changed anything yet. Until I do, I'm no good to any of you—or to myself."

Even though he needed a shave pretty badly and his hair was shaggy, Dad looked almost sure of himself for once. "I'm going to leave tonight," he said. "I'll call for somebody from the joint to come get me. I've been watching you get ready for Christmas. I really don't want to ruin it for you. I don't trust myself, and I have a feeling I should leave before anything happens."

CHAPTER TEN

 ## *December 24*

(*CONTINUED*)

I helped Dad put together the few things he had with him.
I really felt mixed up then. It was a big relief that I wouldn't
have to keep the secret anymore, but mostly I was sorry to
see him go. I wasn't afraid of him anymore, and I think I'd
gotten to know him a little in the past few days. He probably
wouldn't win any prizes, but he was my dad.

Then we got to the top of the stairs, and Ma was standing
in the kitchen waiting. She must have heard voices and
wondered who was in the basement. I quickly put both
hands behind my back, including the one that held the parts
of the music box. But I didn't have to worry. Ma hardly saw
me.

"Monty!" she whispered, eyes widening and hands starting to flicker nervously over her coat buttons. Then she shut her eyes tightly, and I knew she was hoping she had imagined us standing there or maybe she was thinking about going to her room. But after a bit, she opened her eyes, took a deep breath, and I could see she realized she was going to have to walk through—not around—this one.

"Hey, Joy!" said Dad as though this were no big deal. Then he cleared his throat and said, "Well, uh, you're looking good. And, uh, Merry Christmas."

Ma started to say, "And Merry Christmas to you" (which she probably said fifty times a day at work) before she realized how ridiculous it was.

Poor Ma. I quickly explained that Dad had been staying in the basement but that he was just going to call the police to come get him. After that, the three of us stood there, each of us searching desperately for something to say, me trying to look cool with my hands still behind my back.

I noticed two leafy poinsettia plants covered with dark red flowers as big as my face, and said, "Uh, the plants! I mean, where'd you get the plants, Ma?"

It was a dumb question, of course, but she answered absentmindedly, still staring at my dad, "Mr. Lebens let us take home the plants we couldn't sell because nobody is going to want them after Christmas."

I was a little disappointed. I thought maybe she'd finally gotten some Christmas spirit and actually bought them.

But it was my dad who was into Christmas spirits. He had spied the bottle of wine with the red bow that Tyrone's family had sent over.

Ma realized what he was looking at, and her lips thinned. But before she could say anything, Dad said, "Look here. In a few minutes, I'm calling the police. If I don't, you can call them yourself. But it's Christmas Eve, and before I go I'd like to see Christa and Rudy."

Just then, Christa came running into the kitchen. When she saw Dad, she skidded to a stop, eyes wide, mouth dropping open. "Daddy!" she yelled, and then she ran to him. She almost knocked him down, but you could see he didn't mind too much.

She looked up at him, searching his face. I knew what she wanted. Dad hugged her and said softly, "My little sweetheart. My really fine Christa."

I saw my chance and took it. I slipped into the living room and carefully replaced the music box mechanism. Was I ever glad to have that taken care of. I looked up to see Rudy's big blue eyes staring at me with a question in them. Good thing the little guy didn't have a very big vocabulary yet. I picked him up and told him his dad wanted to see him.

And then I almost dropped the kid when he said, "Now?"

"Now"? What kind of a word was that for a "later-maybe" kind of kid?

"Rudy!" I said, "You said 'now'!" He just grinned. I hugged

him. It'd really be nice if there were more "now" people in the house and not so many "tomorrow" people.

Rudy and Dad took to each other right away, especially after we told Dad what a good escape artist Rudy was.

Ma looked thoughtful as she watched Dad with Christa and Rudy. Then she surprised me. She said, "If you're really going back, Monty, maybe the five of us can have dinner together first—I mean, since it's Christmas Eve and all. You can call the police afterward." She didn't say the rest out loud, but I heard it and I know my dad did: If you behave yourself . . .

She looked vaguely around the kitchen. "The only thing is," she said, "I don't know what we've got to eat."

Dad said heartily, "Hey, that's great. I'll fix what we used to have every Christmas Eve when I was a kid. You all go in the other room, and I'll call you when it's ready." Dad seemed happy to have something to do, and of course you could see that he was thinking how he and that bottle of wine were going to keep each other company all by themselves in the kitchen.

The rest of us went in the living room, and Ma read one of Christa and Rudy's favorite Christmas books, *Hilary Knight's Twelve Days of Christmas*, until Dad called us to come eat.

I expected dinner to be uncomfortable. We hadn't been a family for a long time, and I didn't know how we would talk to one another. But it wasn't bad at all. Dad had made fluffy German pancakes, each one as big as our plates, warm and eggy and smelling of almonds. We sprinkled powdered sugar on top, and most of our conversation at first had to do with passing the sugar.

Ma didn't say much, but Dad asked Christa and Rudy lots of questions and even mopped up Rudy's milk. Christa got carried away with the attention Dad was giving her, and I thought she would never stop talking. Dad didn't seem to mind though. Primrose sat on Christa's lap and never took her eyes off Dad. For once, I couldn't tell what she was thinking.

After dinner, Dad patted his stomach and said, "That was great. I think I'll just have a little glass of wine and look at the Christmas tree while I digest those pancakes."

Ma gave him a hard look, but he held up a hand. "Hey," he said, "just a few minutes, okay?"

Although Ma still didn't look too sure, we all went into the living room and sat on the floor around the tree.

But I guess Dad had been on his good behavior for too long. When Ma glanced at her watch after a while, he noticed and said, "Don't be in too big of a hurry to get rid of me, or I might change my mind." Then he told me to get him some more wine. When Ma objected, his face got real tight. I jumped up, although I don't know what I thought I was going to do.

"Looks like it's two against one," he said, looking from Ma to me. "Must be time to go. Why don't you call the police, Nick, and tell them to come get me?"

I automatically headed for the phone. In my mind, I could

see me dialing, talking to the police, hearing the doorbell, watching Dad as he climbed into a police car.

And then I imagined Dad back in prison, talking to the other guys. "Yeah, well, my son turned me in. If it hadn't been for my son, I'd still be free as a jaybird. It was my son who called the cops."

I turned around and slowly shook my head.

Dad jumped up and grabbed my shoulder. "What do you mean, no? Go call the police, I said!"

Ma said to me softly, "He's right, Nick. It's time to call the police. Go ahead."

For once, they agreed with each other. But I thought they were wrong. And it wasn't just because I didn't like being the bad son who turned in his father.

The look on Ma's face stopped me for a minute. Maybe I was the one who was wrong after all. But when Dad turned me to face the phone, I twisted free and said, "No way, Dad. *You* call the police. I'm not doing it for you just so you'll have somebody to blame. It's not me who's turning you in. You decided to go back. You call them."

I held my breath while both Ma and Dad stared at me. I braced myself. What if Dad decided not to call the police after all? Or what if he lost his temper because I crossed him?

When I realized that I had done the only thing I could do, I let out my breath. I knew Dad had to make his own phone call. I wouldn't do it, no matter what he did or didn't do.

Dad had always blamed other people for his "bad luck." If he went back to prison blaming me, or Ma, or anybody else for being there, there was no way he was going to change. Being back in prison would just be one more thing other people had done to him. But if he made the decision himself, it just might get him thinking. He had to start taking charge of his own life, and it had to start happening right now before he left us again. Ma and I were maybe the only ones who knew what he was really like. And this might be the only chance I ever had to do anything for my dad.

Until now, I wouldn't have believed I could stand up to him. And I didn't know until now how much I really knew about my dad.

We must have stood frozen in our places for a good long minute. Even Christa and Rudy were quiet. Like little animals that hide in the bushes when danger is near, they sat half under the Christmas tree, nothing moving but their eyes.

I didn't know which way Dad was going to jump, and I didn't want to move until he did. But just when I thought we couldn't stand the suspense any longer, he walked over to the phone and started dialing.

It took about two years for somebody to come get Dad. I'm exaggerating, of course, but that's what it felt like. Ma silently poured him another glass of wine. I don't think she ever in her life willingly served him anything to drink, and it might not have been the right thing to do, but under the circumstances I wasn't going to say anything. She sat down next to him on the sofa and put her hand over his left hand, which was resting between them. She didn't look at him or anything. Dad squeezed his eyes shut and clenched his jaw. He looked like somebody who's just lost his last hundred dollars.

I was doing kind of all right until I looked at Christa. She had Primrose in her arms, of course. It didn't take a genius to figure out that as soon as my sister let go of her, Primrose was going to head for the cake platter. She had that kind of look on her furry little face.

It was the look on Christa's face that got me, though. Christa hurt. She hurt so bad I just about bawled myself. I whispered, "Dad!" When he looked at me, I nodded my head toward Christa.

"Omigosh," he said. I could see he hated to leave his place by Ma even for a second—that's about how long it took him to scoop up Christa and carry her back to the sofa. He hugged her tightly, saying softly, "My little sweetheart. My really fine Christa." Christa put her head into his neck and sobbed and sobbed.

Rudy was frowning. He never liked it when Christa cried. He probably took in a lot more than anyone knew, but at least on the surface he looked okay. He knew something was going on, but he was too young to get it. We'd have to talk about all this someday, Rudy and me.

What would I tell him about our dad? Maybe that he did the best that he could, which was sometimes kind of funny and wonderful and was sometimes not so funny and won-derful. I suppose it's normal to think more kindly of someone who's going away than of someone who's underfoot and bugging you. I remembered how I had wished Dad would disappear. Now I was wishing—just as hard—that he didn't have to go away. Which was my true feeling? And how could I feel two such different things in a matter of days? Was life confusing, or what?

I watched Dad as he sat there with Christa, and I felt like my chest was going to burst. I was just full of . . . of *stuff* inside. I didn't even know what it all was. I felt sorry for him, of course—sorry because none of his dreams had come true, and sorry because he didn't know yet how to make his dreams come true. Then, too, you'd have to feel pretty sorry for someone facing another prison stretch. The prison part was so awful to me, I couldn't even think about it.

It seemed sad to me that my dad and I had just started getting to know each other, and now it was over. Well, maybe it didn't have to be over. I could write him. And send him clippings from his weird newspapers. He'd like that.

Gabby had always told us that Christmas is a season for giving, that giving is the true meaning of Christmas. Looking at my dad, it all came together for me, how Christmas and love and giving are all mixed together. Because I found myself wanting to give Dad something. I *needed* to give him something. I don't know why and I couldn't have explained it, but that's what I felt. I suppose what I really wanted was to show that I loved him. We weren't very big on saying "I love you" in our family, so I didn't know how else to let him know.

The thought of giving him something had no more than popped into my head when Dad said over the top of Christa's head, "I sure wish I had one of those you-know-whats for a Christmas present, Nick."

All right! In five minutes I was back, with a birdhouse-shaped package tied with Christmas ribbon. He was tucking it under his arm when the doorbell rang.

It took Dad about a minute to give Rudy and Christa quick, jerky hugs, kiss Ma on the cheek, and ruffle my hair. I hardly saw the police officer standing on the dark front porch waiting for him. Then my dad was gone.

When I was younger, I used to chase Christa around the house, pretending to be a monster. She'd run to her room and try to hold the door against me. Of course, I was stronger and always pushed it in, but after a while she learned that just when I was pushing hardest, she could pull the door open and I'd go flying across the room. She loved it!

That's how I felt after my dad left. The door I'd been pushing against had been whipped open, and there I was, sprawled on the floor with the wind knocked out of me.

I wandered around for a while and tried to read an article that Tyrone said was really good—"Santa Claus: Visitor from Another Planet?" But I just couldn't get into it. Christa looked about as unsettled as I felt. In fact, all of us were restless and irritable. Finally Ma suggested that I read to Rudy and Christa for a while.

I started with Rudy's favorite story about the white bear and the trolls who wrecked Christmas. When the trolls squash jellies into the floor, Rudy claps his fat little hands. When they blow bubbles in the milk, he squeaks and honks. But when the trolls paddle in the custard, Rudy really loses it. That's why we never have custard at our house. It's bad enough when he blows bubbles in his milk and squashes jellies into the floor. Nobody is anxious to see him paddling in the custard.

Rudy didn't even notice that he was the only one who was laughing. Christa and I seemed to have lost our sense of humor. I don't know what she was thinking, but I was wishing that Dad could be there to see Rudy squeaking and honking.

After that, I read Christa's favorite book, *The Miracle on 34th Street*. Christa and Rudy complained when I stopped too long, but I couldn't help it when I read, " 'Christmas isn't just a day. It's a frame of mind.' " It came to me that what was still missing for Christmas was the frame of mind. I thought it was understandable. What with Gabby dying and the whole business with Dad, I wasn't surprised we didn't have the right frame of mind. But it seemed a shame.

I went to tell Ma that Christa and Rudy were ready for a good-night kiss. When she opened her bedroom door, I could see a pile of wrapped presents on the bed and scraps of colored paper all over the floor.

My mouth dropped open. "Presents? You've been getting presents?" I said. "When? How?"

She came over to me, pushed my hair behind my ears, and said, "You didn't think I'd leave them around here for you to find, did you? I've been keeping them over at Lurlene's."

"But we thought . . . I mean, we've been watching and you never . . . How could you let us think that . . ."

She seemed to realize what we'd been thinking. She pulled me to her and hugged me. "Oh, Nick," she said softly, "I am so sorry. I never dreamed you kids would be worrying about this." She held me away to look at me. "How could you think that I wouldn't want to get you all Christmas presents?"

I looked away. "Well, you've been pretty, uh, weird lately, Ma."

Her face clouded over. She remembered why she'd been "weird." As she went off to say good-night to Christa and Rudy, I wished I hadn't said anything to wreck her mood. But at least the presents part of Christmas was taken care of. I'd sneak in later and tell Christa she could quit worrying. I should have known Ma would come through, no matter how bad she was feeling. Everything was going to be all right now.

But after I got in bed, I couldn't sleep. I didn't think I'd ever forget seeing my dad walk out the front door like that. I kept hearing him say, "I've broken a lot of things." Was I going to grow up and break things and hurt people, too?

I didn't think so, but how do you know something like that? As I began thinking over the past few days, though, I realized that there had been a few clues about the kind of person I was. I had a temper, yes, but so far I kept from losing it by working on the birdhouses. I think I had more patience than Dad.

Even though I broke the music box, it was an accident. I hadn't broken it in a fit of temper as Dad had. And I didn't *think* I blamed everybody else for my problems. It's hard to know things about yourself, but I thought I took charge of my life pretty well. I'd been working on Christmas for a few days now.

I couldn't remember ever thinking about myself so much before. But lately it had been like Upset the Fruit Basket around our house—first Gabby dying and then Dad showing up and then going away again. I had never had to think about what kind of a person I was, but it seemed important now to figure out who I was.

A new idea started taking hold of me. Maybe I didn't have to be *like* anybody—not like Dad or Ma or even Gabby, although I figured I was most like her. Maybe I was just going to be myself. I guess that would be okay. I didn't know a *lot* about myself yet, but I thought maybe I was okay. Gabby was probably pretty close when she said I was like a border collie—good-natured, hardworking, loyal, and a little bit anxious. What made me think it was okay to just be me was that if I could choose who to be out of all the people I knew—Gabby, Ma, Dad, Christa, Rudy, Tyrone—I'd want to be me. I don't know if that's a good test, but, hey, I was happy with the results.

After that, I tried hard to get to sleep because I knew that the faster I got to sleep the faster morning would come. But something didn't feel right. The house looked like Christmas. We had a Christmas tree and decorations and even five sugarplums. I knew now that we had presents, too. The *things* that we needed for Christmas were all there, but the feeling—the "frame of mind"—wasn't.

I slid out of bed and tiptoed into the living room. I crawled behind the tree and plugged in the lights. As I moved, the tinsel whispered, and the lights were multiplied into thousands of red and green and gold sparkles. I stared at myself—distorted forehead, narrow chin—in one of the red glass ornaments. After a minute, I got up and carefully took Gabby's music box down from the mantel.

Sitting cross-legged next to the tree, I balanced the music box in my lap and cautiously, deliberately, opened the lid. There was a soft whir, and then the seven little angels slowly stood and began to play "Joy to the World."

I could feel a deep sigh coming up from somewhere south of my knees. This was Christmas. The kind of Christmas I remembered. And, yes, it was Gabby's kind of Christmas. I could almost feel her next to me. It wasn't as good as having her *really* next to me, but it was okay.

I heard a noise behind me and snapped around. Ma! She was hugging her bathrobe to her. Her face was in the shadows, so I couldn't tell what she was thinking. I waited uneasily for her to move or speak. When she did, it wasn't what I expected.

She crossed the room, bent down silently, and was suddenly crying softly and hugging me too tightly. I tried to sneak a hand between us to shut off the music box, but she shook her head. She took the music box and rewound it. While she kept one arm around me, she held the music box in the other. We sat very still, listening to the sparkling notes that rained over us like colored fireworks.

I was afraid to move, afraid to say anything. I wanted to explain or apologize. Mostly I wanted to mention Gabby, to say her name, to talk about her. But Ma had never let me before, so I just sat there, glad to have her hugging me.

Cradling the music box, Ma said, "My earliest memory is hearing this play at Christmas. Later, when I was ten or eleven, Gabby told me how it was left with her at the orphanage. I was utterly fascinated. I used to lie in bed at night imagining the grandparents that I'd never seen. I was sure they were rich and famous and had a tragic secret. One day I took the music box apart, looking for a message or for some kind of clue to Gabby's family. I didn't discover anything, of course—except that my mother had quite a temper. I spent the whole day in my room!"

I wanted to keep her talking, so I asked, "What was your favorite Christmas present? Do you remember?"

"Yes, I remember. There are two presents that I'll never forget—both of them the same year. I was nine years old. I knew we didn't have much money that year because Daddy'd been out of work, but when I saw that there were only two presents for me under the tree, I was crushed. Not for long, though! I opened Daddy's first. It was a rock that he'd found, and it was the only one like it I've ever seen. It was almost perfectly heart-shaped. He had polished and polished it and then varnished it."

"Do you still have it?" I asked. "Could I see it?"

"Oh, Nick," she said, "if only you knew how much I'd like to show it to you. I treasured that rock, but I was careless—I used to carry it around with me, and one day it fell out of my pocket. I've never stopped feeling bad about that." She stopped, and I got the feeling that, for her, the rock was lost only yesterday.

She said softly, "Daddy died the next summer. And lately, since Gabby died, I feel as if I've lost Daddy all over again, too."

No wonder Ma had been having such a hard time of it. I didn't know what to say. I waited until she rewound the music box and then said, "What about the other present, Ma?"

"What? Oh, Gabby's present. Well, knowing that this was my only other present, I thought to myself that it had better be good. And, oh! It was. Inside the box was a chubby homemade doll with the sweetest face. Gabby suggested I remove the doll's coat. When I did, I found a dress underneath. And another one underneath that. And under that were sweaters and blouses and pants and nightgowns and, last of all, underwear. The doll kept getting thinner and thinner and the pile of clothes taller and taller. Gabby had made all the clothes herself."

While Ma gently dusted the little angels with the hem of her nightgown, I told her about all the Christmas Eves when I couldn't get to sleep and I'd sneak into Gabby's room. She would tell me stories and sing to me until I was almost too sleepy to stumble back to my room. I let Ma think I had done that when I was a little kid. But the truth was, even last Christmas when I was twelve, I spent Christmas Eve in Gabby's room getting sung to.

I followed Ma into the kitchen while she fixed us mugs of hot chocolate. And all the while she was telling me story after story about Gabby and her dad. They were old stories that nobody had ever told me. Ma talked about Christmas mornings when she was a child, coming downstairs to the smell of raisin-and-dried-apple pies, platters of warm cake doughnuts, and rings of coffee cake. "I can still smell them," she said.

"Gabby tried to teach me to bake, you know," Ma said.

"I remember the blueberry pie disaster. I had blueberries smashed on the soles of my shoes, blueberries all over the kitchen, and a very blueberry smile. The funniest part was that when Mother laughed at the mess, I saw that she had blueberry teeth, too."

I tried to imagine Gabby with her snow-white hair, her neat little rouged cheeks . . . and blueberry teeth. I had to smile.

Ma tightened her arm around me and twisted a little to look right at me. I wanted to look away, but I couldn't. Just try staring right in your ma's eyes from very close up sometime. It's incredibly weird. The only reason it was okay that night was that it was dark and the music box was playing between us and we had been talking about things that we'd never talked about before. So we sat like that, and Ma said, "I love you, Nick."

She rested her head on my shoulder for a minute, and then whispered, "I'm sorry about these last few weeks. I have really been out of it. I noticed you trying to manage things around here, and I knew I shouldn't be letting you do it, but I just couldn't get a grip on myself. I felt paralyzed or . . . or like I was trying to walk through wet cement. Part of me wanted to snap back, to take charge, to let you be a kid instead of the head of the household, for crying out loud. . . ."

She sniffed a little and said, "And I didn't even know the half of it. I had no idea you were also dealing with your father." Her voice tightened a little. "And he is a handful to deal with, as I well know."

"Ah, he wasn't so bad," I said.

I could hear the smile in her voice. "No, he wasn't so bad," she said. "Your father's basically a good man, Nick. He's just got some problems to work out. We all do, I guess. I think you have a pretty good idea of some of my problems—not all of them, but some. I don't know anybody who doesn't have doubts and questions and worries and problems. What would life be like if we were all perfect, anyway?"

Offhand, I would have liked to try life like that for a while, but Ma was older than me and maybe she knew best.

I can't remember now how many times we rewound the music box, but Ma and I sat there for a long time. I have to admit that after a while I got so sleepy I only heard parts of what she was saying. I think she finally noticed that I wasn't paying attention (probably from my snores), and she pulled me to my feet and steered me toward my room. She hugged me and whispered, "It's going to be okay now, Nick." Then, just before she turned out the tree lights, I thought she said, "Merry Christmas, Gabby." I fell, half-shivering, into my cool bed and made a cocoon of my blankets. This old border collie was going to get a well-earned rest!

# CHAPTER ELEVEN

# ✳ *December 25*

Christmas morning was everything I had hoped for. Christa kept saying, "I don't believe it. Santa Claus actually remembered me." Ma only had to dress Rudy once. For Christmas, she had given him a whole collection of zippers and snaps and buttons, and he was obsessed with them.

We went to church, and although I was busy trying not to notice that Pixie Randolph was trying not to notice me, I did wonder about something the minister said. She said that Christmas is about memories, about the past. But it is also about people living forever, people being with us always. That's the way I think of Gabby. I mean, I remember all the things she did and how she was. But I think she's still around—just in a different way.

Afterward, we opened each other's presents and ate Christmas cookies. And all morning long, the music box played from its place on the mantel.

Christa got her loud clothes. There was even a hot pink ribbon and a tiny little green sweater for Primrose. I must have looked surprised because Ma said, "I was a lot like Christa, and I remember how it felt."

And I got my binoculars! Ma had found them at a rummage sale, but the lenses were like new. She also got me my own subscription to *Flying Saucer News*.

Ma cried when she opened the apron from Gabby. But it was a happy kind of crying. Later, she wore it when she fixed Christmas dinner. Personally, I don't think that warming up little cartons from the deli is really cooking, but I have to remember that Gabby didn't have a job like Ma has, so it was easier for Gabby to fix big dinners every day. And sitting around the table together was nice—although I couldn't help thinking of the two people who were missing. Gabby and Dad. Oddly enough, it didn't seem to matter whether they were actually sitting with us or not. They were part of the family. They always would be.

There was a mystery Christmas present wrapped in newspaper and tied with string. It had no name on it, and none of us had put it under the tree. Ma unwrapped it and then put her hand to her mouth. I couldn't tell if she was going to laugh or cry. She held it up.

"It" was a birdhouse. I won't say it was as nice as my birdhouses, but it was close, very close. It took me a minute to see what was different about it: The windows had little tiny bars on them. "Honestly!" said Ma. "That man! What a morbid thing to do." She turned the birdhouse this way and that, and then she laughed. "Oh, well," she said, "why not!"

I was glad she didn't make fun of it. I liked that birdhouse. It seemed important somehow. But today was Christmas, and I was tired of thinking. Give the old brain a rest—that's what I needed.

Later in the day, Peabody stopped by with candy canes for everyone. Just before leaving, Peabody said, "C'mon, you guys, tell me the truth. Which one of you is Leon?" We all burst out laughing. I think we sounded a little rusty at first, but as I listened, our laughter mingled with the silvery notes of "Joy to the World" to make the very best kind of Christmas music.